In the Himalayas
A Sage from Assam

In the Himalayas
A Sage from Assam

Prankrishna Kalita

PARTRIDGE
A Penguin Random House Company

To order additional copies of this book, contact
Partridge India
000 800 10062 62
orders.india@partridgepublishing.com

www.partridgepublishing.com/india

Contents

Dedicated

To my departed parents

PREFACE

In the Himalayas, a sage from Assam is the English version of the Writer's original popular novel in Assamese (*Himalayat Ajan Asomiya Sanyasi*). This is transformed by the writer himself to English. There are some difficulties in translation work from Assamese Language to English. It is found easier to translate into Indian Language from English. Some unrelated portions of the original novel have been omitted in the English version.

In the creation of literature, there does not exist age-bar, but needs inspiration from own self or from others. The writer does not know how far he has been successful in the translated version of the novel in English. Readers will judge this. Besides the story, there is related description to the shrines. In the novel there remains the unification of imaginations and realities. It would be better to call the present book, 'A social and religious novel.' The writer will be happy, if the readers accept the novel.

M/s Partridge India are thanked sincerely for taking responsibility of publishing the novel.

July, 2015   Prankrishna Kalita

Chapter-1

This is Rishikesh, full of beautiful natural scenery. It is a place of study centre for the Hindu religion. There are many *ashrams* (religion retreats), religious study centres, temples, centres for study of philosophy. Also there are centres of Yoga, the quasi religious practice which is exercises to remain healthy on the basis of Hindu Philosophy.

Regarding the name of Rishikesh, there are some stories. Rishik means wisdom. It means master or chief owner of wisdom and mind, which actually means God. Addition of two words has formed the name 'Rishikesh'. It is said that great sage Rishav had practised severe penance on the bank of the Ganga. Being pleased in Rishav, the God appeared before him in guise of a sage named Rishikesh. And thereby the name of the place went on as Rishikesh.

In the past Rishikesh was the holy abode of many sages and gods, so it is believed.

There are four main religious shrines for the Hindus in the Himalayas, which are called *'dhams'*. Those are the Badrinath, the Kedarnath, the Gongotri and the Yamunotri. For pilgrimage to those four *dhams*, Rishikesh is the gateway, being the foothills of the cloud kissing Himalayas.

Now a days Rishikesh has grown up as place for tourism. There are many pilgrim houses in the temples for pilgrims. There are hotels, tourist lodges, rest houses for the tourists. There are modern schools and colleges. There are Rishikunda and Raghunath temples, where Lord Sri Ram bathed, it is believed. The Chandrabhaga rivulet falls in the Ganga here. Tribenighat is where rites are performed for the peace for the soul of the dead by Hindus. It is believed, in the past there were two other rivers, the Yamuna and the Saraswati besides the Ganga which is presently flowing. Thereby the place had been named Trivenighat, union of three rivers.

Lakshmanjhula is three kilometers away from Rishikesh. It is said that Lakshman, brother of Lord Rama, made the *jhula* (bridge) to cross the Ganga river. In 1939 the bridge was made with iron ropes. There is Swarga Nibash (Heaven's abode) nearby where big temples are there. Fourteen kilometres away from Rishikesh there is the temple of Mahadeva, the blue necked God. Nearer to this temple, there are the temple of goddess Bhubaneswari and Jilmi caves.

In the Manikut hill, there is the Kailashnanda *Ashram* (shrine). A little away from Swarga Nibash, there are Swarga *Ashram,* Gita *Bhavan* and Paramartha *Niketan.* Also there are Sibananda Ashram, meditation shrine (Yoga Centre) of Mahesh Yogi, Puskar temple, Satrughna temple, Satyanarayan temple etc.

....I was sitting on the bank of the Ganga at Tribenighat, enjoying the pleasant sights of the nature. I was catching cold. I thought to take a bath in the holy water of the Ganga. But the colour of the water had become turbid, probably, due to erosion of earth in upper hills. Up to Lakshman Jhula the Ganga river is narrow. From there it becomes somewhat wider. And from Rishikesh it flows to Haridwar. From Haridwar the Ganga flows through plains and meets the Yamuna river in Prayag (Allahabad). And thereafter it flows few hundred kilometres to fall at the Bay of Bengal.

I was hesitating to take bath in the muddy water. Suddenly I heard a deep male voice saying 'Don't worry. All the water and earth of the mother Ganga are pure". I turned back and saw a sage with flowing hair, was going fast. I saw his backside but could not see the face.

I decided to take bath in the earth-coloured water of the Ganga. I took bath for some time in the cold water. Changing my cloths, I sat down for few minutes on sunny sand. I felt better and coldness vanished from my body. Words of the sage came to my mind. I thought, it is the grace of the Ganga.

Taking my bag on back I walked unmindfully on the bank. After little distance, I have seen two holy men with saffron cloths. They were smoking hemp in small earthen bowl. I sat beside them. One of the holy men offered me to smoke but I refused. He asked me with a keen look, where from I had come. I told him that I had come from Guwahati, Assam. The other holy man uttered,

'Assam!' After that he said very enthusiastically, 'You are from the land of goddess Kamakhya. I know one sage a little from your Assam. I have seen him this morning for a while. He travels four *dhams*. Sometimes he comes here also.'

Suddenly it came to my mind about the sage who crossed me little while ago and told 'The water and land of the Ganga are pure.' I asked the holy man,

'Where does the sage stay here? Can you tell?' The holyman replied, 'He may stay in the *ashram* of a temple at Rishikesh. Or he may stay at Lakshman Jhula or even at Haridwar also.'

I asked him, 'In which *ashram* the sage may stay, can you help me to find out him? Do you know his name please?'

He replied, 'Here the holymen are not known by their names generally. Very few are known by their names. All are known as *Babaji* or *Swamiji*. It is difficult to find out someone by name. We know only seeing their faces. Who will know whom in this

Himalayan region! Very few of Babajis or Swamijis have known address to find out.'

— 'Is there any way to find out the sage from Assam?'

— 'You can try in the shrines or *dharmasalas* (pilgrim houses) of the temples.

— 'How I can find him out? I know nothing about him. If you help, I can try."

— 'You can try, but do not expect much from the nearby *ashrams*.'

On my request one of the holymen agreed to help me. I hired an auto-rickshaw. Both of us had moved and after a while we arrived at an *ashram*. The holyman who was with me, went inside the *ashram*. Returning he said 'In this *ashram* the sage is not available. He is not staying here.' Our auto-rickshaw started and moved to another *ashram*. I wanted to see the sage from Assam once! My companion entered another *ashram* to find out the sage. But he returned with no hope. Taking a deep thought he said, 'Let us go to that temple.'

Our auto-rickshaw started to continue our search. After reaching the temple, my companion went inside the *ashram* of the temple. I was sitting in the auto-rickshaw waiting for him. I was looking the sight of the temple. After about half an hour the holyman returned with a smiling face. He said to me, 'You are very lucky. Swamiji from your Assam has been found.' I was very glad to hear the news.

The driver of the auto-rickshaw was told to wait for us. We entered the *ashram* to meet Swamiji. On the way to *Dharamshala* of the temple, I said to my companion, 'You have taken pain for me very much. Thanks a lot. I may be late. Will it be inconvenient for you?'

He said, 'I shall go away after you meet Swamiji. You will talk to him as much as you like?" I had paid the fair of the auto-rickshaw to him with some extra money.

He took me to a room. He made me acquainted with Swamiji who was sitting on a mat on the floor. He said 'Swamiji, this person is from your Assam, who is eager to meet you. We met on the bank of the Ganga.' I greeted Swamiji with folded hands. Swamiji was looking at me deeply for a while, then said to me.

'Please, take your seat'.

I sat on the mat. I had noticed, Swamiji would be few years younger to me. With long hair and short beard his was face. Keeping his book on the floor, he noticed me deeply again. The holyman who accompanied me, left Swamiji and me. Swamiji asked me, 'Brother, when did you arrive at Rishikesh?'

I said, 'There was my departmental work for a week in New Delhi. From New Delhi I came to Haridwar yesterday. After visiting Haridwar for the whole day, I arrived at Rishikesh in the evening.'

'Which place in Assam do you belong to?' He asked me.

'I am from Guwahati.' I replied.

After uttering 'Guwahati' he thought something. Then he asked me, 'Have you come alone? After Rishikesh where will you go?'

I said, 'I have come alone. After this I shall go to Dehradun and Mushouri. I had come here once before.'

Swamiji said, 'Is it not difficult to travel singly?'

I said 'Yes, there are difficulties, but we have to travel.'

He kept himself silent for few minutes. Then he asked about my name, address and occupation. I replied in short.

He said, 'You are in central Government service. You have no shortage of money to acquire religious merit by donating and subscribing to temples.'

I tried to understand what actually Swamiji had wanted to mean. I replied,

'In fact I have no habit to donate to temples or other religious institutions. I do not want to purchase virtues. The incomes of temples are many lakhs of rupees in the name of religion in India but there is no proper utilisation of those money. The so-called holymen of many temples and shrines maintain lavish livelihood with all modern facilities. In many temples, the priests are troubles for pilgrims and visitors. I have not said about all temples.'

Swamiji said, 'Yes, now-a-days general people are reluctant to visit many shrines for pilgrimage. They are in fear and suspicion. Rich people, ministers and highly placed officials do not have to wait for visiting temples, in queues. Special entrances are open for them. Now, in the name of religion, many immoral activities are prevailing. Those who offer fat donations, become special category of people.'

I said, 'We should make amendments of some laws regarding religion.'

Swamiji said, 'In the name of religion, there are anti religion acts. Who will prevent all those sinful deeds? Everywhere you will see malpractice and corruption. Had not Mahatma Gandhi's hope of the 'Ram Rajya' (an ideal realm) vanished with his death? In the past, India was land of learned sages but now people are hankering after earthly enjoyment. Mahatma Gandhi's political party also has abandoned his ideals. All want power at any cost. Mahatma Gandhi did not want partition of India. In political twist, India was partitioned. Death came to Mahatma Gandhi and other leaders got enjoyment of power.'

I said, 'Political parties seek to get power. Politics is now a play of money and muscle. I am unsatisfied with the religious trusts' work culture. Incomes of the temple-trusts are few crores of rupees, with the donations of educated and illiterate people. Officials and spiritual guides collect large amount of money and gold. Now-a-days a good magician can be a spiritual guide in the name of religion. It is a good business.'

He said, 'We have deserted preaches of our religion. At present our people have forgotten to worship Sri Ram or Sri Krishna. They worship particular spiritual guides. They donate a part of their just income. There is no limit of donations by the dishonest and the corrupt".

I said, 'Not only our religion alone, in the world all religions play the game of money. The Christian states of the world donate a large portion of money to the Pope's state of Vatican City. Those countries are secular then why so much money are spent in the name of preaching of a religion! I do not speak of India as a whole, but in Assam Christian missionaries have opened many schools. Ulterior motives of opening the schools are preaching of Christianity among the poor people. Governments do not bar these activities. Because, ours is a secular country!'

Swamiji said, 'Do the rich Muslim countries not supply money to our Muslim institutions? India was divided on the basis of religion. Pakistan became Muslim country. India became secular country. It did not become a Hindu country. If you go to the past, you will see how are the Hindus were oppressed. History is the witness, how the Mughal emperors except Akbar, behaved with the Hindus. We are secular country but there are different laws to rule in the name of religion. World's only Hindu country, Nepal is approaching China, for these wrong policy of India."

I said, 'After the Mughals, there came the British to India. Thousands of Hindus became Muslim in Mughal period. In the British rule period, Christian preachers got a vast country. Again, how many thousands of Hindu became Christans! Who will obstruct this stream?'

Swamiji remained silent. No sign of manifestation was on his face. I had not asked him anything till now. I thought he might get hurt, if I had asked about his past life! Leaving behind his home and family, he was living in these Himalayan places! He might feel uneasy, if I had asked something! I should not ask about his private life. Yet I asked him, 'Swamiji, for how many years, you have been living the life of a sage?'

He replied with a deep voice, 'Brother, in true sense I have not been able to become a sage. Actual sages meditate in penance severely. They want to search the very existence of the God. They become very powerful spiritually... I have spent some years in this present way of life. Meeting with you today, is a concurrence. It was to meet you. You wished to meet me heartily. Here you will get different types of holymen and monks. All of them have been living here, leaving their pasts. Some might have come on their own. Some have come falling in the circumstances. The 'swamis' or 'babas' here or in other religious shrines are not only Hindus, there are from other religions also. Their identity is same as 'swami' or 'babaji' or holymen. It is the union place of pilgrims for all. Now-a- days many facilities are there in shrines of temples. There are *'Dharamshalas'* or charitable trusts. Many of holymen live on alms. The water, the land of the Ganga and the climate of the Himalayas keep them all healthy.'

Suddenly it came to my mind the incident, when he said about the water and land of the Ganga. When I was waiting on the bank to take a bath in the water of the Ganga, the very sage said, 'The land and its water of the mother Ganga are all pure'. The voice was like that of Swamiji! I uttered, 'Swamiji, do you remember Assam?'

He remained calm and quiet for a while. His eyes were towards the outside. After a thought he said, 'One old memory has come to my mind, Asom Gana Parishad party had formed the government in Assam, after the Assam movement started by All Assam Student Union (AASU). After wining in election and forming the government they did the first work- increase in pay scale of ministers and legislators. They had forgotten to take steps to drive away illegal immigrants. The results of giving power to the inexperienced youths was pathetic. For their own selfishness, they had kept the old experienced people at a distance. I think sometimes, had then Chief Minister Lokpriya Gopinath Bardoloi lived for some more years! He served Assam selflessly. Mahatma Gandhi thought to do many important works for India after getting freedom. That did not happen. Bardoloi also wanted to do many things for Assam– that did not happen...

I said, 'Ministers and legislators of the Asom Gana Parishad (AGP) government, did not take into account wise and learned sections of the people of the state of Assam. They had forgotten the basic obligations to Assam. AGP came to power. They failed. Again Congress Party govt. came to power. There were no concrete policy and principles. AGP and Congress, all are same. They have no time to think for the welfare of Assam and the Assamese. All are blind to power. AGP came to power for the second time. Situation of the state remained same, no improvement was there. Ministers and legislators did not correct themselves. They became arrogant and haughty like the people being rich suddenly. They had neither wisdom nor idea to understand the mental agony of people. Again Congress came to power. Situation of the state remained same. Peace did not return to the people. People in power, have same nature, they run after riches and lavishness. They have no time to redress the sorrows, flood-afflictions and hardship of people. Unemployment is a big problem in the state. No government gives importance to solve the problem. Ministers and legislators have become family oriented. They do not feel shy of being corruptible. Money for development vanishes in corruption. AGP government could not give protection to people. Congress government also could not. AGP had lost goodwill of majority Assamese. But the love for the religious minority remained same for the congress. The dream shown by AGP to the people to make golden Assam, disappeared in air. There is no recruitment officially, but the recruitment by backdoor goes on in departments through bribery. But the AGP and the congress governments had given one dangerous present to the people of Assam– open wine shops and wine bars. It has done severely harmful effect to young students of schools and colleges and to the society as a whole'.

Swamiji said, 'Where will you get leaders like the ones of the past Congress in the Centre or states? The images of the past chief ministers, ministers and legislators were clean. Time now has changed. People also have changed. Everyone wants wealth by any means. They are not afraid of sins and crimes. They do not know that, death is waiting for them. Sooner or later, death will come to them one day. King Harishchandra of great Surya dynasty had to be beggar after donating everything. Now-a-days many people have become modern 'Harish' of wealth of immoral earning and malpractice. Ill-gotten money given in donations, does not bring blessings, rather, brings sin doubly. People in power get scope to amass wealth. Who will prevent them! It is an anti-religious act in the name of religion. Place of honesty in society has come low. The wise are harassed by dishonest people who are in power.

Now-a-days it has become difficult to get justice. Sinful days are coming!'

I said, 'You have cited the former chief ministers of Assam! Bishnuram Medhi and Sarat Chandra Sinha were honest, devoted and true Gandhians. An experienced journalist wrote series of discourse regarding former chief ministers of Assam. He criticised these two former honest chief ministers bitterly. The act of the journalist hurt people. He ridiculed late Bishnuram Medhi in his writings, for being childless. Regarding Mr. Singha the journalist wrote, he was offered tea in a cup of cheap quality. How did this aged journalist dare insult those two respected former chief ministers? It shows the wicked mind of the journalist. He perhaps, forgot the ethics of journalism. Now-a-days newspapers are full of government and private advertisements. Even halves of first pages of the news papers are full of advertisements for the greed of money. Publication of newspapers is a big business now.'

Swamiji uttered, 'The writing of the journalist had certainly hurt others. To me the journalist had self interest here. At present it is difficult to get selfless and impartial journalism in true sense. This particular journalist, perhaps, sought favour for himself, someone of his family or for newspapers in which he worked during the days of the two chief ministers. He did not get favour and hence he wrote that way in malice. Certainly this is against the true journalism. If you see from the point of psychology, it shows the selfishness of the journalist. Want of courtesy is everywhere.'

Swamiji asked me, 'The All Assam Students Union (ASSU) did lengthy agitation to drive out illegal immigrants from Assam; what did happen at last? The then government did not heed the movement seriously. On the other hand the government wanted to crush the movement. An Assam accord was signed. But how much was Assam benefited by the Accord?'

I said, 'Socially no benefit came, but politically some benefit came. After the movement Assam Gana Parishad (AGP) party was formed and they got political power after the election. The central government officials laughed at the ASSU leaders for poor fluency in English. The officials did this deliberately to disgrace the student leaders. Late Lal Bahadur Shastri did not pass Matric exam even. He devoted himself for freedom of India. But he became the Prime Minister of India. Late Gyani Zail Singh also did not pass Matric exam either. But he became the President of India. If the higher education and fluency in English are necessary to be leaders, then why those leaders and economists with degrees of Harvard University and London School of Economics have not been able to remove poverty of the people of India after so many years of freedom? Whatever degrees they may have, but where will we get persons like Gandhiji and Shastriji who understood the inner sorrows of the hearts of people of India? AGP got power in Assam. Mr. Mahanta became chief minister. He did not try to understand the voice of people of Assam, he was busy in getting university degrees.'

I stopped for a while. Swamiji was also silent. Again I started, 'Not only Mr. Mahanta but other ministers also forgot to perform their duties. Certainly they had deficiency of knowledge and wisdom. Gandhiji felt the soul of India, hence he was called 'Mahatma', the noble soul. Mr. Mahanta got golden chance not only once but twice to understand the voice of Assam. Being blind to power, he failed to feel the spirit of Assam. Had he been able to avail the chances, he would have been the Mahatma of Assam. That Mr. Mahanta is now fighting for his very existence. Another minister, one day, was traveling with a senior bureaucrat of the state government in a car. The young minister was smoking cigarettes heavily inside the car and puffed the smokes towards the bureaucrat. Feeling insulted, the bureaucrat afterwards had left his loving Assam forever. Being in power the young ministers became haughty and arrogant. Pride goes before a fall, let it be either AGP or Congress government. Chief ministers and ministers of Congress governments also do not try to understand the voice of people. This hurts me badly.'

Swamiji said, 'Avarice of government official and leaders, their incompetence and blindness to power bring disasters to the people. The party in power thinks only for the people in their party in states or in the centre. A government should be unbiased for development of all people as a whole. Every citizen of the country has the equal right in development work. After getting power once, the party and the government try to return to power again. The expenditure of fund is done, keeping in mind for vote-bank. This is an injustice to the people in general. Power makes leaders blind. How many do leaders get inner thoughts of happiness doing good to the others? Opposition parties criticise the government, this is a normal process. The governments in power, can't tolerate criticism. They are want of courtesy and good manners. Leaders with security provision around them feel unsecured. Disraeli said, 'There is no gambling like politics.'

I began to think, in what way Swamiji might think about myself! I thought to be careful in dealing with Swamiji. My one or two careless words may hurt him. He may take me otherwise. I have come to conclusion–'Swamiji is a learned person having different knowledge at this age.'

I was surprised when he asked me suddenly 'Was not during the tenure of AGP government in Assam, the United Liberation Front of Assam (ULFA) born?'

'Yes', I admitted meekly. There was silence. I thought, why he was asking me this question! Was he connected with ULFA in any way in past? May be or may not be! I should not suspect without any reason. Curiosity came to my mind.

Breaking our silence he asked, 'How far did the organisation succeed for freedom of Assam? Do you know anything?'

I could not find my words to reply to him. After a pause I said, 'Certainly you are talking about ULFA. Deaths came to many youths during students' movement in Assam. After that, there came the rebellion by ULFA. To continue the rebellion, they needed more money. They established camps in foreign country. Insecurity prevailed among the people of Assam. The governments also did nothing. Today also it comes to my memory of the small town. There were some big rice mills in the town. Amongst them there was one which was very big. In my boyhood I was astonished seeing lofty store houses of rice mills. Now the rice mills are no more. The organisation (ULFA) demanded huge money from these mills. The owners had fled after selling the mills in cheap price. They did not get security from police. Many industrial establishments were closed down for the fear of ULFA. Death came to many people. ULFA wanted money to buy arms. They coerced people for payment. Those who did not pay money, were murdered cruelly. They invested money in foreign country for business also.'

Swamiji was listening to me silently. I continued, 'Then army was deployed in Assam. Death came to many ULFA cadres. In the name of ULFA, there came death to many innocent people. People had to suffer from the unknown fear- psychology. Army is in one side and ULFA in the other side. There were other rebellion groups also other than ULFA. There was uncertainty everywhere. When and which group made explosion of bombs, no one knew. It was not surety for people going out for work in morning, whether they would come back in the evening. Some ULFA cadres took shelter forcibly in villages. Villagers could not complain fearing retaliation by ULFA cadres in one hand and harassment by army on the other hand. All governments remained as meek spectators. The voice of government was– 'the power and energy of ULFA have come low.' Thinking about these, I am feared – 'future of Assam, security of people– everything is in the hands of the God.'

Swamiji was seeing to my face. Then he said, 'It is a relief to speak the voice of heart. You are one eye-witness of the happenings in Assam. ULFA had certainly collected many crores of rupees. With the only money power and arms one cannot win a battle. For that, they should have brave warriors, have expertise in leading and competent management. Without knowing how much powerful they are, they should not think of weakness of the enemy. It was foolishness to ULFA. So many deaths came without any reason. The Nagas were engaged in battle for the freedom of Nagaland against central government of India. Their demand for free Nagaland had some legitimate reason also. Indian government did not agree. Army was deployed in Nagaland. At that time allegations were that, Naga grown up girls and women were physically and sexually tortured by army personnel. People of Nagaland were suffering badly. The leaders seeking freedom of Nagaland were shattered in pain seeing the oppression to the people. And the demand for free Nagaland became weak. Indians got freedom from the British. But Indians could not get sharpness and competency of administration of the British. Those old laws and acts are prevailing with new faces in power only.'

More curiosity came to me hearing Swamiji's words. I was listening to him carefully. He again began to speak, 'Tamil rebels had waged armed mutiny against Sri Lanka government for its cause of a free Tamil state. Getting a free Tamil state, it is not expected that fantastic developments would come for Tamils. Some states in Africa got freedom. But today see their conditions. Civil- strife, fight amongst themselves for power, blood-shedding are happening in those states. Indescribable sufferings of people are going on. I have taken the Tamil issue to compare ULFA with LTTE (Liberation of Tamil Tiger Elem). Panic stricken ministers, government officials and businessmen paid money to ULFA. Even now they are paying. LTTE cadres also exhorted money by coercion. They also got money from sympathisers. They also purchased arms and ammunitions. Their camps were in Sri Lanka itself unlike ULFA. LTTE cadres even attacked the President or the Prime Minister of Sri Lanka. They were successful in many cases. Captured LTTE cadres took poison capsules which were kept with them readily and thereby committed suicide. Exploiting female cadres, the LTTE had succeeded to kill a former Prime Minister of India. They blackened the competency of intelligence branches of the Centre and states of India. How many captured cadres of ULFA did commit suicide? Can you say? Rather, many ULFA cadres surrendered to police and army easily. All deaths, murders and suicides are very painful. These should be stopped.'

I was listening to Swamiji heartily. I tried to speak something. I said,

'There is another story. Government lured the ULFA cadres. They caught the lure and many cadres surrendered meekly. Many surrendered cadres got provision offered by the government. But now other horror and terror came to people. The surrendered cadres did not obey any rules. But the government tried to make people understand that many cadres had come to the main stream of people in Assam. But people were scared of terror. The surrendered cadres thought that they had come out with big win from the battle field. In fact they had done blunder. They should have behaved like law-abiding citizens. Had they done so, people would not have laughed at them saying 'fugitive, coward army-men.' Some surrendered cadres got facilities from the government, but the rest got nothing. Some cadres began to cultivate on land. Government kept many surrendered cadres in camps. Those cadres have been kept in camps leisurely without any work or duty. They are paid monthly stipend even.

Government's version is that 'ULFA organisation is now very weak.' Only unseen God knows the fate of Assam and the Assamese!'

I observed Swamiji with interest. He was looking towards hills through window, keeping his right hand on his head. Breaking silence after a while he said, 'Will a second Mahatma Gandhi be born in India? Many people think that Gandhiji's ideals are old fashioned today. He brought independence to India by non-violence. What did he get in exchange? How much respect he got from the Indians! Horrible communal violence occurred in the eastern and western parts during the period of partition of India. In those difficult times Gandhiji without fearing death, went to the oppressed people in east Bengal. Then Prime Minister of independent India, Mr. Nehru approached and requested the foreign Governor general of free India, Lord Mountbatten to take steps to control the spread of terrible communal violence. Ungrateful Lord Mountbatten sought the transfer of the reign of full power to him even for few hours. At the sacred moment of birth of freedom, what a mortification of subjugation! Due to strong determination and opposition of Mr. Ballabh Bhai Patel that power was not transferred to Lord Mountbatten. Gandhiji did two mistakes. First, he did not appoint Mr. Patel as Prime Minister of India. He appointed Mr. Nehru. Had Mr. Patel been made Prime Minister of India, the shape of democracy and administration of India would have been different. In the name of democracy the taking over of power would not have happened like dynastic rule of monarchy in India. Today not only in centre, many states of India have rush for dynastic rule in power.'

I said, 'I support your views. Members of parliament (MP) and members of legislative assemblies (MLA) win in election for their strength of money and muscle. They even do not fight shy to ridicule honest candidates. MPs and MLAs after getting power, become less worried for sorrows and grievances of people.

This is a farce and an insult to the democracy. But Swamiji, you have not mentioned the second mistake of Gandhiji.'

With a smile on his face he said, 'Second mistake of Gandhiji was that he did nothing for his family. Seeing the distress and sufferings of poor Indian people, Gandhiji spent ordinary and arduous life. On the other hand Mr. Nehru was luxury loving. Today, leave the ideals of Gandhiji, do you see even a photo in news papers on the day of his birth or death anniversaries? Gandhiji observed fast in jail. He thought all the time for freedom movement of India. Mr. Nehru was busy in writing books and letters. Mr. Nehru's relationship with Lady Mountbatten was known to the people.'

The atmosphere of the shrine (*ashram*) is peaceful. At the evening, temples would be illuminated, sound of conch-blowing and bell will be heard. After taking a glass of water Swamiji said, 'Instead of religion, we have discussed politics. Actually you know, you cannot get rid of some past memories of incidents though these might happen years ago. Whatever you try to forget, those memories come and disturb your mind. Everyone is affected by the happenings in life more or less. Some incidents of childhood or grown up age affects severely afterwards. Some people forget slowly but some cannot forget even by efforts. Had any such incident happen in your childhood age or afterwards?'

I was silent for a while. He was waiting for my reply. I said, 'Certainly some incidents happened. But two of them bring disturbance to me. Old ones, but those remain in me living and gives sadness in my mind.'

Swamiji wanted to know regarding incidents. I began to narrate the first incident, 'I was four or five year old child. I had a little sister. Her name was Phuli. My mother named her lovingly. She was one and half year old. One day she was playing in varandah. Accidentally she drank kerosene oil from the lamp which was lying there. I was nearby. She was coughing. My elder brother and sister took her immediately to the village dispensary. The doctor was not present. The compounder was there. Phuli was administered some medicine mixing with water by the compounder. She was sleeping on my mother's lap. Slowly Phuli's body began to be pale. Some people in the dispensary said that firstly vomiting should have been done to Phuli so that the kerosene oil comes out from her stomach. But the compounder answered that the medicine given to her would do well. I was seeing all the happenings. The compounder was from our same village. Phuli did not survive. She died after few hours. Many people said that due to wrong medicine dispensed by the compounder, Phuli died. After her death a pathetic scene was seen in our home. My mother cried and cried for some days. I had been weeping. I did not go to the dispensary till the compounder was there. I was scared to see the compounder. Whenever I saw him on road, I wanted to strike him with piece of stone. I hated him from the corner of my heart. One day I saw my elder brother was talking to him. I angrily said to him, 'Why do you talk to the compounder?' My elder brother perhaps understood my emotion. He remained silent. After two years the compounder was transferred to other place. I was the happiest boy hearing his transfer. I wanted his death, not transfer. I thought, 'Why God does not punish the compounder who is the cause for my sister's death. This incident happened in my childhood period, but I could not forget. It hurts me even now.'

Swamiji looked at me deeply. I became very emotional. He offered me a glass of water. Then he said, 'It is pathetic to lose loved one. At the death of your little sister, you suffered a lot mentally and your hatred for the compounder is natural. It hurt deeply you in childhood days. You mentioned another incident, please tell regarding that incident also.'

I tried to be normal. I started to tell my second incident. I said, 'The incident occurred when I was a high school student. I was in class IX. Our Headmaster Sir cared for studies to students. He was a resident of our nearby village. We knew him as the founder Headmaster of our high school. He was very sharp in English. He studied in the famous Cotton College in Guwahati. He actually came as founder headmaster. But he did not return to his original service. He could not leave the school for love and affection of students. He tried his best for the development and good result of the school. He was a true Gandhian. He put on spotless white *khadi dhuti* and shirts. He was known to many ministers and high officials in state government. When we were in lower classes and afterwards also, big leaders and ministers visited our school. When I was in class V, once the great socialist leader Mr. Hem Barua came to visit our school. Some students of us were waiting. He came to us and said, 'Small boys.' He was chewing betel-nut. A small silver-container with betel-nuts was by his hand. 'You spell the word 'intelligent' very fast,' he said. I was in front of him. I became very nervous. Yet I spelled the word very fast correctly. Headmaster Sir came fast towards him. Mr. Barua calling his name with smile told him, 'Your small students are intelligent.' Smile came to the face of the Headmaster. We were very happy to get a chance to speak to Mr. Barua, the respected leader. Though our Headmaster was a Congress man, he kept good relations with other non-congress leaders also.

When I was in class IX our headmaster alerted us for studies. He said to us to be attentive and careful for studies only. He even warned me of deducting my monthly scholarship money if I got less than 80 percent marks. My elder brother was a teacher in our school. The headmaster also told me that he will enquire regarding my studies from my elder brother. He warned us telling that after two years matriculation (HSLC) examination would come there. Therefore, we had to be serious in studies. Without good marks we would not get admission in the Cotton College.

For appointing new teachers the meeting of Managing Committee was held. We heard afterwards that hot and bitter debates went on in the meeting regarding appointment of a candidate of a particular member's choice. The Headmaster and some other members of the committee objected the candidature. For, the candidate's education qualification was very poor from Matriculation onwards to graduation degree. The candidate passed examinations with very poor marks. The Headmaster pointed out that if a candidate with such poor result was appointed, the standard of education would be low. In past also some members of the committee tried to grudge him with false allegations, saying that he was not from our village. But the people of our village stood behind the Headmaster. Then those members could not succeed in their plan. Those members urged the committee to appoint that particular candidate even though his results were bad. The Headmaster and other members opposed strongly.

After two days when the Headmaster was returning home at evening, some miscreants attacked him. When the residents of nearby houses came out, the miscreants flew away taking cover of darkness. He was wounded on his head. But he was speaking. Doctor came only early morning next day. Doctor declared that wound was serious and he should be shifted to Guwahati Medical College Hospital for urgent treatment. Police arrived and took statements. Our headmaster told the names of five miscreants including two members of the managing committee. He was taken to Guwahati for further treatment. Chief Minister of Assam declared that all possible treatments would be given to him. In the mean time his condition was going bad to worse. The Chief Minister again assured that criminals would be severely punished. The case had been taken by the government.

Strike began at school with the demand for the arrest of the culprits. The Headmaster fought between life and death for three days. Then came the agonising news, the death of our Headmaster. The government again assured for swift action and judgment. But the police did not find out the culprits till then to arrest them. Police's version was 'efforts and investigation are going on.' Dead body of our Headmaster arrived in school compound. Condolence meeting was held. Students and villagers wept quietly with utmost sorrow. What could they do except weeping? That scene was painful and agonising.

Two months passed. The atmosphere of school was completely different. No teacher was for mathematics. Two or three good teachers left our school and joined in other schools. No one wanted to come as Headmaster to our school. My elder brother began to talk less after the incident. No more our Headmaster was to alert us to get admission in the Cotton College getting good result in HSLC exam. No more our headmaster was to warn me to stop my scholarship money, if I got less than eighty percent marks!

When I was in class X, after few months news came one day that due to absence and non-availability of witnesses, the culprits were acquitted. New assurance from the Chief Minister had come, appeal would be filed to the higher court against the present judgment. People understood, nothing would happen. The case should have been fought by themselves instead of the government. Certainly result of the judgment would have been different. All knew that police had taken money from the culprits and the case was fought weakly. It was heard that the government advocate also did not fight the case sincerely. People expressed angrily, there was unethical link amongst government pleader, advocate of the guilty and judge. If not, why then 90% cases fought by the government are defeated! Temptation of greed for money makes them very low and mean.

The culprits roamed in the village shamelessly without bodering to feel the sentiment of the villagers. Whenever I saw someone of them, all the hatred came out from mind towards, but I could not do anything. Alas! Our system of law and justice! Our law is to punish the guilty or to acquit the guilty! It came to my mind– government's assurance, advanced treatment, acquittal of the guilty– all these are farce. Police made the case weak taking bribe from the guilty. Knowing all these I suffered a lot. Thinking of the incident, gave tremendous mental shock to me. I tried to forget but could not. Why our beloved Headmaster was murdered? The faces of the culprits, I felt, made me frowned. Are the laws, courts, lawyers, police, ministers able to give justice to the people in true sense? All these institutions laughed at me!

Facing a little courage, I prepared to sit in HSLC examination. Memory of the Headmaster came always and felt disturbed. Examination was over. Result also came out. Though I did not get high percentage of marks, I passed in first division with the letter marks in mathematics. We were three who got first division and were admitted in the Cotton College in Guwahati with science stream. I thought, 'The soul of our late Headmaster got at least some solace thinking that we got admitted in the famous Cotton College. We tried to forget the dark past. But in Cotton College Hostel, senior students made reference and asked regarding the murder-case of our late Headmaster. It gave agony. Again the memory of our Sir brought grief to us.

There was deep silence between me and Swamiji. He observed me inquisitively. Breaking silence he said, 'The incidents happened in your childhood and boyhood certainly affected you mentally.'

To change the context Swamiji said to me, 'Some interesting incidents might happen in boyhood period. Memories of those incidents may give pleasure to you even today. Tell me one or two regarding such incidents?"

I thought– Swamiji perhaps wanted to change the context to give a lighter atmosphere between us. I tried to memorise some light and interesting happenings in my early life.

I told, 'In my boyhood life some interesting incidents happened. One cousin and myself were good companions. He was one class lower to me. In one half yearly examination he was beside me. He was weak at arithmetic. After the examination result it was found, he got 80 percent marks in that subject. The teacher called him to explain how he got such high marks. The teacher also asked whether he copied in examination. He said the truth to the teacher that I had helped him in examination. The teacher had doubt. The boy who did not do well, this time how could he get such high marks in that particular paper! The teacher called me why I helped my cousin in examination. One teacher said, 'Had he got 10 or 20 marks more, no suspicion would have come to us. But he got marks more than 80 percent.' All the teachers were laughing. As it was our first time fault, we were pardoned with a warning that if in future such wrongs were done by us, severe action would be taken. The incident gave amusement to others for many days.

That cousin and myself were interested in catching fish. Whenever getting any opportunity, both of us went outside to catch fishes. Fishing net and creel were tied with the bicycle, we rode. Extra towels and half-pants were also taken to change the wetted ones in catching fishes. Every year shoal of fishes came in our nearby river. To catch fish was our hobby but in shoal it was more interesting and a special one to catch fishes. I did not attend school for three days. On fourth day when I attended, the assistant headmaster entered class. Before calling our roll-calls, he observed students. Seeing me he said sarcastically, 'Being the first boy of the class X if you do not attend class, it would be better for you to admit yourself in lower primary school. Give fish to teachers and your attendance would not be necessary. Roar of laughter was raised in the whole class. It was big embarrassment for me in presence of my class-mates. My head bowed down in shame. Then the teacher said gravely, 'Examination is nearby, be regular in attendance in class.' The application which I brought with me giving reasons that I was suffering from colic pain, was not submitted. There was an unwritten rule for all students that whenever they were absent themselves in school the reason was given as colic pain, though other reason might be there. I knew that our teacher came to know my absence for catching fishes from my elder brother.'

Smiles returned to Swamiji. He said, 'Our lives are full of smile and weeping and happiness and sorrows. Life is itself a mystery. Mental sufferings and hazards make people experienced in life; accumulates energy to live.'

Again he told, 'In the battle field the strength of army is known. This does not mean that battle is run to examine the strength of army. In past the kings and ministers fought battle to protect the people. Commanders and soldiers got inspiration to fight without fear against enemy. There is no king now in our country. There are president, prime minister, ministers, chiefs of army, air force and navy. No need to fight by themselves against enemy. They only collect information. To fight there are cadres under them. Win gives credit to top brass and defeat gives discredit to lower rank holders. Some questions came to my mind......

India was defeated by China in 1962 war. Then Prime Minister of India Mr. Nehru gave consolation speech to people of Assam thinking that Assam had gone to China's hand. Minister of defence tendered his resignation. But the President or the Prime minister did not resign. The President is the supreme commander and the Prime minister is the supreme administrator of the country. Would our country not run if they had resigned? Ours is a democratic country, not monarchy. Questions may be irrelevant, but are these questions irrelevant actually? Then President of India, Fakharuddin Ali Ahmed allowed the use of loud speakers in mosques. Day and night many times religious messages are announced from mosques. These are actually political appeasement. Oh! Our democracy! In departments there are some criteria and qualification for appointment of candidates. There are interviews and tests for candidate in writing and orally. The appointments of the President, the Prime minister, chief ministers, ministers, governors are done by political parties. No age limit is for them. Is there any system to evaluate their credibility and competency? Is there any guarantee that they will do their duty impartially or selflessly?'

After a pause Swamiji again said, 'In old days soldiers along with king and ministers who lost their lives in battle field, got the honour of hero-worship. After death their journey was to the heaven. Now-a-days the Heads of democracy cannot get 'hero-worship', for no necessity to fight in battles by them. Those warriors, who lose their lives in battle-fields, get heavenly abode. They dedicated their lives for the cause of motherland. Only they have the right to get such type of honours. Their deaths are immortal. Their souls go to the heaven. I do not know actually whether there is the heaven or the hell. People get peace for the faith of religion. The souls of your little sister and the headmaster are living in the heaven. The souls of the culprits who murdered your headmaster would remain in the darkness of the hell. Thinking this way, you will get solace in your mind.'

I was listening to Swamiji solemnly. After a second thought he again started to say, 'Many great sages by their utmost persistence unveiled many mysteries of the nature for the cause of wisdom and truth of the soul. Present science of nuclear energy, relativity and sound-waves has got great advance. But it is surprised to think that in past great sages like Narada, Vyas, Agusta and many more availed unlimited power and strength of wisdom. Those were certainly not imaginary. They got phenomenal emanation and was able to know about distant ones by producing wave energy. Many sages of the past acquired divine grace and got the knowledge of the past, the present and the future. Therefore, they were called 'Trio-time wisdom' (*Trikalajna*). Present science has acknowledged that human brain can produce waves. Present science has done great research regarding soul.'

It came to my mind that Swamiji was a learned man. He might study different kinds of books. He had acquired knowledge not only in religious matters but other fields also.

Chapter-2

I said to Swamiji, 'You have perhaps gone for pilgrimage of 'four shrines' (*char- dhams*), Badrinath, Kedarnath, Gangotri and Yamunotri and other places many times. I have a great desire to know about these four *'dhams'*. I shall be very happy if you tell me something regarding those holy places.'

Swamiji began to describe– This Himalayan region is called the heaven in the earth. White peaks and green mountains have created the great scenery. According to 'vedas', the holy scriptures this region was called Sapta Sindhu (seven seas) in past. These Sapta Sindhus were Dhalganga, Vishnuganga, Mandakini, Nandakini, Pindar, Bhagirathi and Nayar. Big rivers were called Sindhu (sea). The Vishnuganga was also known as the Alakananda. In *'Scanda Puranas'* (ancient religious book) it is found that the place where the main stream of the Ganga and river Nayar united, was called Sapta Samudrik (seven seas) pilgrimage.

Distance to four *'dhams'* from Rishikesh is more or less about two hundred and fifty kilometers. Add or subtract ten or twenty kilometres this way or that way. Amongst four *dhams,* Badrinath is called the holiest one. Height of Badrinath is more than ten thousand feet from sea level. By bus journey from Rishikesh you will get Debaprayag- Srinagar--Rudraprayag--Karnaprayag- Nandaprayag--Chamoli--Gopeswar--Yoshimath--Vishnuprayag--Govindaghat. From Govindaghat you are to walk six kilometres to reach Badrinath. Now-a- days small vehicles run to the *'dham'.* Badrinath Temple stands on the bank of the Alakananda. The Badrinath Temple is also called as the Narayan Temple. On east there is Nara mountain and on the west Narayan mountain. On the back there is Nilkantha mountain range. Near the Badrinath the river Vasundhara falls in the Alakananda. Here is the Vashundhara waterfall. From eastern side at Govindaghat the Hemganga rivulet joins the Alakananda. Before Govindaghat, you will get Vishnuprayag and Yoshimath. Yoshimath is covered in three sides by icy mountains. There is the Trishul mountain in the south, Kamet mountain in the north and Badrinath mountain in the west. From Govindaghat, Ghagaria is fourteen kilometres away in the east and to Hemkunda lake another five kilometres. Hemkunda lake was discovered in 1932 by a devotee of the Golden temple of Amritsar, called Bhai Chohan Singh. There is saying that the founder of its Khalsa sect, Sriguru Govinda Singh first meditated on the bank of the Hemkunda lake as a sage. Here is the Gurudwar (Sikh Shrine) called Hemkunda Saheb. It is believed that taking bath in this lake, pilgrims get rid of accidental and untimely death. At a distance of five kilometres from Ghagaria there is the valley of flowers, the National park. Height of this valley is more than eleven thousand feet above sea level. In 1931 mountaineer Frank Smli discovered the valley of flowers. From Gobindaghat the distance is 19 kilometres to the park. During July and August months whole valley is bloomed with different flowers of a thousand varieties. The scenery of the valley with flowers makes the nature incomparable.

At Vishnuprayag the Dhauli river falls in the Alakananda from the east. The Nandakini river falls at Nandaprayag in the Alakananda. At Rudraprayag the Mandakini river coming from Kedarnath falls in the Alakananda. At Debaprayag, the Bhagirathi river coming from the Gongotri, joins with the Alakananda and flow together taking the name Ganga towards plain. There is Srinagar in between Debaprayag and Rudraprayag. It is believed that God Vishnu worshipped Lord Shiva at the temple Kamaleswar at Srinagar with one thousand lotuses and gained the Sudarshan Chakra (Throwing Disk) from Shiva.

Meaning of Badri is wild plums. In the past the place was full of Badris. Near the main Badrinath temple, there are other four temples. Together five it is called Pancha (five) Badrinath. The main Badrinath temple was constructed by Adi Guru Sankaracharya in eighth century. There is a saying that Lakshmi Devi (goddess of wealth) taking the shape of a plum tree bestowed shadow to meditating God Vishnu. Lord Shiva-devotee Ghantakarna kept a bell on his ear so that except Shiva he did not hear other god's name. Lord Shiva bestowed a boon to Ghantakarna to get emancipation; but Lord Shiva also said to him that only God Vishnu could bestow him actual emancipation. Ghantakarna then began to worship God Vishnu keeping his body under water. God Vishnu bestowed a boon to Ghantakarna and gave him the place in Badrinath temple as the caretaker. According to scriptures it is said that no one would get peace of mind and soul without pilgrimage to the Badrinath. The temple of Badrinath is fifty feet high. Badrinath temple is also called Badrinarayan temple. The statue of God Vishnu in temple is made of black Salagram stone. The statue is in the form of meditating position of God Vishnu. There is hot water spring in Badrinath. The temple was damaged many times by severe sleet. It was repaired time to time. The temple remains open from April to November months. The holy lamp in the temple remains enkindled during the closed months. The statue of God Vishnu is taken to Yoshimath for those closed months. To stay in Badrinath there are pilgrim-houses, tourist lodges. There are facilities for pilgrims to stay in temple shrines.

After this Swamiji went on to tell about Kedarnath *dham*. He described -- Kedarnath *dham* is the abode to Lord Shiva on the bank of the river Mandakini. To arrive here you are to go by bus on the way-- Rudraprayag-- Augustamuni- Ukhimath--Guptakashi--Sonprayag. From Rishikesh to Rudraprayag the road is same to Badrinath and Kedarnath *dham*. From five kilometres distance from Sonprayag there is Gourikunda. From Gourikunda it is fourteen kilometres away to Kedarnath *dham*. There is bus-running road from Chamoli to Ukhimath. From Sonprayag you are to walk 19 kilometres to Kedarnath dham. Mules and porters are available. Kedarnath is one of the twelve sacred phallus images of Lord Shiva. Kedarnath *dham* is at 11500 feet above sea level. It is a holy place for pilgrimage for the Hindus. Lord Shiva is the God to destroy evil deeds. Meaning of Kedar is powerful. The Mandakini river is flowing from the Cherabari glacier which is five kilometres away from Kedarnath *dham*. At Sonprayag the river Vasuki falls in the Mandakini. Mandakini means, flowing silently and bestowing peace.

There are some springs at Kedarnath *dham*. Those are Shivakunda, Retkunda, Hansakunda, Udarkunda, Rudhikunda etc. At Gourikunda there is the temple of goddess Gouri. At nearby Chitrakut there is the temple of goddess Anusuya. There is the temple of Bhairabnathji.

Lord Vishnu came to the earth for the well-being of mankind. He arrived at Badrinath. At that time Badrinath was the abode of Lord Shiva. On request, Lord Shiva shifted his abode to Kedarnath allowing Lord Vishnu to remain at Badrinath. It is said that after winning the Kurukshetra war of the Mahabharata, Pandavas came to the Kedarnath *dham* to worship Lord Shiva to get solace for murdering relatives in the war. There are five temples in the Kedarnath *dham* and nearby areas. Those are Kedarnath temple, middle Maheswar temple, Tunganath temple, Kalpeswar temple and the Rudranath temple. In winter seasons the Kedarnath faces heavy snow falls and remains closed during November to May. There is a saying that when temple remains closed for months, Bhairabnathji protects the Kedarnath temple from evil-doers. Snow-fall at Kedarnath *dham* creates an unparallel sight. Those pilgrims who see the moon in the sky of the Kedarnath *dham* are very lucky. Moon-lit nights with snow-covered peaks and mountains produce an imaginary light. It is believed that if death comes to someone in the Kedarnath *dham* he or she approaches Lord Shiva straightway. It is said, the way to the heaven begins at Kedarnath *dham*. Pandavas of the Mahabharata started from here to ascend to the heaven. The statue of Lord Shiva is brought to Ukhimath during winter when the temple is closed down for pilgrims.'

Swamiji stopped for few minutes. Then again he began. He said, 'The road to the Gongotri from Rishikesh by bus is Narendra

Nagar-- Chamba-- Tehri-- Dharba-- Uttarkashi--
Gangani-- Longka--Bhaironghat. From Langka
you are to walk eleven kilometres to the Gongotri
through Bhaironghat. Gongotri is situated at ten
thousand feet above sea level. The Ganga is flowing
from Gomukh of the Gangotri glacier. From
Gongotri to the glacier Gangotri the distance is
19 kilometres. The height of the glacier Gongotri
is more than twelve and half thousand feet from
sea level. There is the temple of the goddess Ganga
at Gangotri. The temple was constructed well by
Gorkha Commander Amar Singh Thapa. Pilgrims
offer worship here so that rebirths of their ancestors
do not happen again. The Ganga is known here as
the Bhagirathi. The Bhagirathi after flowing through
Bhaironghat, Gangani, Uttarkashi and Tehri falls
at the Alakananda at Debaprayag. After flowing
through hills and mountains the river goes to the
plain taking name the Ganga at Debaprayag. The
natural scenes seen on the way to the Gongotri are
fascinating.

There is a story that in the past there was a king
named Sagar. The king killed many demons. Once he
wished to perform the ceremony of horse-sacrifice.
From his first wife, the king had several hundred
sons. From his second wife he had only one son
called Ajmanchas. Indra, the king of the heaven had
feared seeing the bravery of king Sagar. Indra feared
this time thinking that if the ceremony became
successful king Sagar might attack the heaven also.
King Indra hid the horse of the ceremony in the

shrine of the sage Kapil. Sons of king Sagar went to search the horse. They arrived at the shrine. Sage Kapil was at that time meditating. Feeling disturbance the sage was very angry with the sons of king Sagar. He cursed them. They were burnt to ashes. Somehow Ajmanchas's life was saved. He came back and informed the king Sagar everything.

Anshuman the grand son of the king Sagar went to sage Kapil and was able to take back the horse. The sage also told him that goddess Ganga had to come to the earth from the heaven and then only souls of sons of the king Sagar would get solace and emancipation. Anshuman did not succeed to bring goddess Ganga to the earth after many efforts. Even his son king Dilip also failed. At last his son Bhagirath was determined to bring goddess Ganga to the earth. He began to perform ascetic practice in the place called Topovan on the glacier Gongotri. Many years passed. At last gods became soft to Bhagirath. They agreed to bestow boon to Bhagirath with the condition that he can ask for only one boon. Bhagirath asked for one boon that, goddess Ganga must come to the earth. Goddess Ganga was angry when she had to come to the earth after leaving the heaven against her wish. In the heat of anger goddess Ganga began to flow in such a ferocious speed that she would destroy everything on her way. Seeing dangerous form of goddess Ganga, Lord Shiva stopped the flow and kept in his matted hair. Again Bhagirath began to worship Lord Shiva devotedly to satisfy him. At last Lord

Shiva was pleased and allowed to flow three streams of water from his matted hair. One of the streams began to flow following Bhagirath who was blowing conch, with the flow of water to the shrine of sage Kapil, where sons of the king Sagar were perished. Due to making flow of the Ganga to the earth by Bhagirath, the Ganga also is called the Bhagirathi. The flow of water of the Ganga liberated the souls of sons of Sagar for salvation. In the place of the rock sitting on which Bhagirath worshipped Lord Shiva, the Yodhaganga or Jahnabi rivulet joins with the Bhagirathi. It is said that the roaring sound at the descent of the Ganga to the earth, disturbed the sage Jahnu in his meditation. At the heat of anger, the sage drank all the water of the Ganga. After the earnest and humble supplications of Bhagirath, the sage Jahnu allowed to flow the water of the Ganga through his knee. Jodhaganga is called the daughter of the Sage Jahnu. Therefore, Jodhaganga is also known as Jahnabi. Actually Jahnabi is a tributary of the Bhagirathi. Here the natural scenery is fascinating and charming.

At the distance of seventeen kilometres from Topoban there is Bhabishya (future) Badrinath after crossing the Dhauliganga river. It is also said that one day the roads to the Badrinath would be destroyed and ritual performances would be done at this Bhabishya Badrinath. In Gongotri there are the Surya Kunda (Sun pit) and the temple of sage Parashar. Parashar was the father of sage Vedabyas. Pandavas came to the Gongotri. They offered sacrificial rites for the Salvation of their relatives who were killed in the Kurukshetra war. There are guest houses, lodges for staying of pilgrims at the Gangotri. Accommodations are also available in *dharamsalas* of the temple. Pilgrims bring the holy water from here to their homes.

At Uttarkashi there is Nehru Institute of mountaineering. At Tehri the river Bhelongana falls at the Bhagirathi. This Tehri where the construction of heavy dams has been constructed for producing electricity at the cost of crores of rupees. The government is showing dreams to people saying that not only *Garwal* region but all other places of the state would get vast development with prosperity. The dam is a merciless blow to the nature. In fact, not the people but the contractors, ministers, bureaucrats and multinational corporate houses are to be benefited. They will keep their corrupted money in the banks in Switzerland or St. Ketis! This is a ghastly fraud to the people.'

After this Swamiji stopped for a while. I could not ask him anything. I only supported him silently. He then started to say about Yamunotri. He said,

'Yamunotri is the abode of the goddess Yamuna. It is near the Bandarpunch mountain range. Actual source of the flow of the Yamuna river is the Saptarshi lake of the Champasar glacier in the Kalind mountain. Natural scene of the whole Yamuna river valley is very charming. Yamunotri is situated at ten thousand and five hundred feet above the sea level.

There are two ways to go to Barkat from Rishikesh. One is Rishikesh- Dehradoon--Mushouri--Campfalls--Kuwa--Nagaon--Barkat. Other is Rishikesh-- Narendranagar--Chamba--Tehri--Dharba--Barkat. From Barkat you use to proceed to Chayanchatli--Hanumanchatti-- Phulchatti--Janakichatti--Yamunotri.

From Hanumanchatti you are to walk thirteen kilometres to reach Yamunotri. On the way you will get Phulchatti and Janakichatti. Yamunotri is six kilometres away from Janakichatti. From Hanumanchatti there are two ways to reach Yamunotri. One is through holy site Markendeya and another through Kharsani. Markendeya holy site is the place where great sage Markendeya composed Puranas, the Hindu mythological scriptures. At Hanumanchatti horses and porters are available for the pilgrims. At Yamunotri there is the Surya-kunda (Sun pit) of warm water and also Gourikunda. At Janakichatti there is the Taptakunda (hot pit) of hot water. Hot water spring Dibyasila is presented to the goddess Yamuna by her father god Surya. From Suryakunda there is hot water flow to Taptakunda, where pilgrims take bath. Before worshiping at the main temple, pilgrims worship first at Dibyasila. Goddess Yamuna was said to be the eighth queen of Sri Krishna. On the day of the ceremony of Yanmastami (birth day of Sri Krishna) feet of the statue of Sri Krishna is washed with the water of the Yamuna river. Pilgrims take holy water from the

Yamunotri to their homes. In the 19th century king Pratap Shah of Gorwal built the temple properly.

The source of flow of the Yamuna river is the Saptarishi (seven sages) lake which is ten kilometre away from Yamunotri. It is said that Brahma-padma (supreme spirit lotus) blossoms at the lake. There is a story regarding the goddess Yamuna– The god Surya (Sun) married Sanjadevi, the daughter of god Vishwakarma. Sanjadevi could not bear the heat of the sun easily. Their son was Yama and the daughter Yamuna. Sanjadevi could not see the god Sun eye to eye. Being unendurable, one day Sanjadevi made a facsimile of herself naming Chayadevi. Sanjadevi left the home of the god Sun. Before leaving she told Chayadevi not to disclose the secret to anybody. But Chayadevi kept one condition before Sanjadevi. The condition was that she would disclose the secret if god Surya punished her some day pulling her hair. Sanjadevi agreed before leaving. One day son Yama kicked his mother (duplicate mother) with leg. Then Chayadevi at the heat of anger cursed Yama that he would be diseased and his legs would be detached from the body. God Sun was at wrath to her for cursing Yama heavy punishment for a light fault. He dragged Chayadevi pulling her hair. Then she disclosed the secret to him that she was not the true mother of Yama.

Yamuna returned to the earth and on the strength of meditation she made Yama curse-free. Yama asked her to take boon from him. Yamuna took the boon asking that her devotees should not die accidentally ever. From then it is believed that whoever takes bath at Yamunotri, he or she will not die in accident and they will get solace.

Distance between the Gangotri and the Yamunotri is seventy kilometres. They are called sisters. After flowing through different places for one thousand kilometres the Yamuna joins the Ganga at Prayag (Allahabad)

Devotees to *Char-dhams* (four shrines) should keep warm clothes. Some may suffer in breathing. They should take medicines. There are guest houses, shelters for staying in shrines for devotees.'

After taking a glass of water Swamiji again said, 'It will remain incomplete, if I do not tell about the Manash Sarovar (lake Manash) of Kailash (abode of Lord Shiva) in the Himalayas. The lake was created from the mind of Brahma (supreme spirit). In the Sankha Scriptures it is written—'nowhere in the earth likes of the Himalayas are found. Morning sun dries dews and by the same way, the sight of the Himalayas purifies human sins.'

The Kailash peak is at 21,700 feet (6677 metres) above sea level. According to the scriptures of Hindu Puranas, Buddhism and Jainism the Manash Sarovar is the centre of the universe. Manash Sarovar is below the Kailash mountain at the height of more than fifteen thousand feet (4690 metres) from sea level. Depth of the lake is three hundred feet (91 metres). Total area of the lake is 320 sq. kilometres. Four rivers have come out from the lake. From the north the Indus, from the west the Sutlej, from the south the Karnali and from the east the Changpo comes out. The Changpo after taking the name Brahmaputra has entered the north-eastern India. On the west of the Manash Sarovar and on the north of the Kailash there is another lake called Rakshasthal lake. There is water stream in between the two lakes.

Kailash is the habitation of Lord Shiva and his consort goddess Parvati. It is the holiest place. It is believed that drinking the water of the lake and taking bath here, devotees get freedom from the bondage of rebirth. After the death, their souls go to the heaven, it is believed.

China government had closed since 1949 to 1980 the pilgrimage for the Indians to the Manash Sarovar. In 1981 they opened for the Indians for traveling.

Indian government notifies for the travel and pilgrimage to the Manash Sarovar.

Those who want to travel are to go through some rules and regulations.'

Swamiji again said, 'In India, states have different cultures and languages. In the name and faith of the Hinduism people in thousands come to the *Chardhams* for pilgrimage every year.'

After he completed I said, 'I am very much benefited knowing all about the *Char-dhams*– Badrinath, Kedarnath, Gangotri and Yamunotri. You have everything in memory about the four shrines and the Manash Sarovar.'

Swamiji said to me, 'You also try to go once to the *Char-dhams*. You will get a big experience in your life. I asked you about the culture and language in Assam. What about the Bihu festival of Assam now-a-days.'

With some efforts I replied, 'Today our Bihu culture is dominated by modernity. You will get variety shows in Bihu stage. Stage for Bihu festival is not a cultural show in the true sense. It is a way to get entertainments only for the people now. Very little number of committees only have kept the actual virtues of the Bihu festival. In most of the Bihu festival committees, it is seen the president is not even matriculate. Doing brokerage, business of land deal they have become rich. People make them president or secretary only seeing their money. In the stage when wise and educated persons are seen with them, it gives pain to many people.

Swamiji said, 'At one time ULFA talked vociferously regarding Assamese culture. Why then they do not object about the depleted culture of Assam? The government has started wine shops and open bars. Why do ULFA not demand closure of those shops and bars? It is written on the label of bottle 'drinking is injurious to health'. And it is written on cigarette packets 'smoking is injurious to health'. Why then do the governments not close sale of wine and cigarette, if it is injurious to health?

The government itself applies dishonest methods to collect money.'

I remained silent, I could not find out words to speak. It was about to be evening.

Swamiji again said, 'After a short while worship will begin at the temple. So much time has been spent in discussion of different topics with you. I make myself a little fresh washing my hands and face.'

I said, 'I want to take your leave today. Tomorrow I shall come again to meet you. At what time will it be convenient to you, please?'

He said with a smile, 'I think, you will not leave me. I shall be free at 10 AM to 11 AM. You can come at that time.'

I left Swamiji bowing my head.

After leaving Swamiji I rested myself for some time on the bank of the Ganga before going to hotel. Electric lamps began to light in the town. Temples and shrines were lighted. Uniting all these, the scenery had become very beautiful. Sounds of bells and conches came from the temples. After washing my face with the water of the Ganga I returned to hotel.

When I reached hotel, the Garwali hotel- boy enquired of my departure to Dehradun. I said,'For my different engagements in Rishikesh my departure is postponed now.' I asked him to send tea and biscuits to my room. After entering my room I washed my hands and feet. I felt somewhat easy. The hotel boy brought tea. I covered my body with the woolen blanket and sat on bed. Sipping tea I thought about the events of the day. I was enchanted by Swamiji with his conversation. My curiosity regarding Swamiji began to increase. Swamiji's citation of Mahatma Gandhi, Assam, Tehri dam, description of *Char dhams*, *Manash Sarovar* in Kailash– all these took my mind to an unknown place. More questions and doubts arose to me. Conditions of our people have remained poor even after so many years of independence! What we have got in the name democracy! It is difficult to win an election without money and muscle power. In what way are we going with the multi-parties political system? Prosperity of a country is compared to the standards of improvements of living condition of people. Increase of big buildings and costly cars on roads do not show the true picture of development. Differences between the rich and the poor in India are alarming. The poor are struggling for two meals a day. The governments in power have introduced schemes for supplying rice to the poor at a low price or freely spending crores of rupees. But the major benefits go to the middle men illegally. Laws cannot catch those evil forces. Ministers also give protections to them. It is a farce in the name of the poor. Motive is only to win elections. The poor should be engaged even in small works by the government. So that they understand the dignity of labour. Supply of free rations to the poor cannot improve their living conditions, rather it makes them idle. They should be engaged in some cottage industries. Government should take care of the diseased and the old. Government should take responsibility of education for children.

Governments are keeping reservation quota for the scheduled castes and scheduled tribes in education and employment from the independence period. The provision was initially for ten years. But the governments and political parties have kept the provision till today for their vote-bank politics. The creamy layers of the scheduled castes and the scheduled tribes also do not want to lose the benefit of the reservation. The reservation system should be removed and there should be only one reservation policy for 'the economically backward people' of the country and not on the basis of castes and creeds. Then only we can get rid of evil effects of caste-system in India. In India it is a surprise to see the politics in the name of the poor and castes.

I thought regarding the Tehri dam Swamiji said. How mush the common people are benefited in general! Few thousands of megawatts of electricity are produced. For whose interest! It is an injustice to the nature's creation. It has destroyed the charm of the nature for human selfishness. It fears me– one day the Brahmaputra river valley would be destroyed by the greedy government! Governments boastfully declare about the increase of the national production rate. But without the prosperity and development of the living standard of the mass, is the shouting of the increase in production rate any meaning?

Population of China is more than that of India. They are developing equally for the people. At the same time, they have made tremendous rise in science and technology, socio-economic field, military science, commerce etc. India is under developed in many fields. Real cause of backwardness in India is malpractice and corruption. The convicted ones for corruption in China are sentenced to death by firing after completion of judgment within six months. In India judgment does not come for years. Indian judiciary is strange!

Asom Gana Parishad government could not expel illegal immigrants from Assam. Congress governments are silent in the matter. The ULFA cadres should come back to mainstream of Assam. They should take steps to to help to expel illegal immigrants from Assam and fight against corruption and injustice.

In Assam army and police men tortured the innocent people in the name of searching for secret money of the ULFA. Swamiji also referred regarding Bihu cultural festival of Assam. It came to my mind–Bihu festivals are no more of the past. Now-a-days Bihu festivals are money oriented shows and open use of alcohol has discredited the culture. In India only one or two states have restrictions in sale of alcohol. Why the other states do not stop sale of alcohol! Actually states want more taxes selling poison to the people. In Assam if corruption and malpractices are stopped in Chagolia and Srirampur check posts, the government can collect many times of taxes than that of selling alcohol to the people. But that is not done, for the government wants to continue malpractices and let people die drinking alcohol. Prostitution in India is illegal. As per government's version, there are many lakhs of prostitutes in Indian cities. Like the writing on the labels on bottles of wine 'drinking is injurious to health', the governments can make prostitution legal with writings in brothel as 'whoredom is injurious to health.' And the government can collect more taxes.

In the midst of my thoughts the hotel boy brought meal for me in the room. After taking meal I went to sleep with the thought to know more about Swamiji next day. I got up at 6 A.M. and was walking in the verandah. I was delighted to see the sight of the morning at Rishikesh. I decided to see some places at Rishikesh and Lakhmanjhula before I went to Swamiji. On the way I would take something. I took the sweater in my bag, which was purchased in New Delhi.

First I arrived at the bank of the Ganga. Sitting there I thought– 'so many stories are there related to the Ganga.' Starting from the Gongotri in the Himalayas and flowing 250 kilometres through mountains and green forests, the Ganga reaches Rishikesh. After Rishikesh the Ganga reaches Haridwar and flows few hundred kilometres in plains to fall at the Bay of Bengal. Great poet Kalidas in his immortal and excellent poetic works described the Himalayas as incomparable specially cited in the Meghdoot, Sakuntala and Raghubansha.

In 1929 Mahatma Gandhiji came here once. Seeing the beauty of the Himalayas from here he remarked, 'Hospitality of the nature enchants all here.

There are boundless beauty, enchanting greenery and the superb environment in the Himalayas. What can a man expect other than these? I do not think, anywhere in the world such types of treasures of beauties are available.'

Certainly the mountains, hills, peaks, rivers, tributaries, rivulets and green vegetation have created the united treasure of beauties in the Himalayas. Pain and distress of the body and worries and woes of mind are relieved here. An unknown happiness brings enjoyment to body, mind and heart.

I dipped in the water of the Ganga to take bath. Today the water is clean. After swimming for some time in the water I came to the bank. After changing clothes I walked to road. Hiring an auto-rickshaw I visited two or three temples in Rishikesh. After this I moved to Lakhmanjhula through the road on the bank of the Ganga. After paying fare to the auto- driver I crossed the river walking through the hanging bridge. I visited three temples at Lakshmanjhula. I did not go to other temples thinking that I might be late to reach Swamiji.

I took two breads with curd in a small hotel. Hiring an auto -rickshaw I started to move to the temple shrine at Rishikesh, where Swamiji was staying. It was 11 AM. After paying fare to the auto-driver I hurriedly walked to Swamiji's room.

Chapter-3

Swamiji was sitting in his room. I entered the room with a salutation to him with my folded hands. Before Swamiji said something I spoke, 'I went to Lakshmanjhula to visit some temples in the morning. Hence I am late to reach you.'

'For how many days you will stay at Rishikesh?' He asked me.

I said, 'Actually my program was to go to Dehradun even yesterday. Spending two days at Dehradun and Mushouri, I was to return to Delhi. My advance ticket to Guwahati was booked. But now I have decided to return to Delhi from here itself. I want to know about you more, so that my curiosity ends here.'

Swamiji had observed me and remained silent for few minutes. Then said to me, 'Wishing to know about me, you have reminded me of my past.

Thoughts cannot be shared with all. Everyone may have some secrets, but these can be disclosed to or discussed with favorite persons only. You have impressed me though I do not know why. I shall disclose and tell you about myself.'

...After this Swamiji began to tell the story of his life. He went on to narrate in his own words......
'From the famous government college at Guwahati in Assam, my friend Apu and myself passed Higher Secondary Examination with good results. Apu wanted to study Medical Science and I in engineering. We spent time discussing different subject- matters. Apu's elder sister was Aru. Actually sister Aru's name was a long one. The name was shortened to Aru. And for Apu and me 'sister Aru' became 'Aruba' in short form. Aruba also joined in our discussion sometimes. She was a meritorious student. She was a student in final year of degree science having major in physics.

I said to Apu, 'If you become medical doctor, try to research in medicines to make white of black skins of people.'

With a smile in her face Aruba asked me, 'What will you do after being an engineer?'

I replied, 'If I become a civil engineer, I shall plan to construct a bridge on the Brahmaputra without pillar in the middle of the river.'

Apu said loudly, 'If the bridge breaks down!'

Aruba remarked, 'If adulterated cement is used, the bridge would break down. Without adulteration, how would the ministers, contractors and engineers be benefited?'

All of us got laughter. I said to her, 'You have spoken the truth. Then I leave civil engineering. If I do the mechanical engineering, I shall try to invent a device to find the end point of the universe. Aruba, you are a student of physics, you are to help me.'

Again laughter roared. Aruba said, 'Firstly get admitted, then speak about invention. Do you not know, the incompetent also get admissions in the medical and engineering colleges through back doors?'

After ending all speculations, Apu got admission in medical college and myself in engineering college. Before sifting to college hostels, one day we were discussing about something leisurely in their house. I said, 'Many people believe in superstitions. Our society and scientists should take steps to remove blind faiths from our society.'

Aruba said, 'You are very right. Take for examples the lunar and solar eclipses. Many people in the world including in India believe that the eclipses are divine acts. In India many people believe that demon Rahu swallows the moon and the sun and therefore eclipses happen. Many people do not know and die without knowing the factual acts of the eclipses. The earth moves around the sun and the moon around the earth. When the earth comes in between the sun and the moon in a straight line position, the shadow of the earth falls on the moon. Thereby lunar eclipse happens. In the same way when the moon comes in between the sun and the earth, the rays of the sun are blocked and thereby solar eclipse happens. Eclipses may be partial or total. There are other eight planets of the sun other than the earth. There are many lakhs of stars in the universe. Regarding the eclipse, superstitions in people can be removed even from the illiterate people by showing simple visual documentaries. When sodium metal comes into contact with water, it catches fire. Magicians make people fool by showing that, they can produce fire from water.'

Apu said, 'Many people think that suffering from diseases is the act of the God.'

I said, 'Some organisations should come out to remove blind faiths of the people. Governments have no time to think about these. This blind faith of the people till their death is a pathetic picture of the society.'

After one week Apu shifted to his medical college hostel. I also shifted to the engineering college hostel. In hostel I had seen a different field. That field was the ragging culture to new comers by some senior students. I hated some of the senior students, for their ragging methods and low mentality. Somehow I managed but conditions of the hostel mates of my class were miserable. I consoled myself thinking that the ragging masters of senior students, were mentally diseased and sons of mean families. My hostel mates got some relief seeing my courage to bear the onslaught of notorious ragging in college hostel.

After few days I met Apu and had come to know that he also was a victim of ragging. I told him to suppose them who ragged badly as mentally sick. Future of many talented students has been destroyed being the victims of ragging in different colleges in India. Our society, governments and College-authorities have failed to take severe actions against ragging in colleges.

Apu and I did not inform at our homes regarding ragging. We feared that our families might get hurt in mind hearing these. We thought that particularly, Aruba might be worried.

First year had ended and I was promoted to second year. Apu also was promoted to second year. Aruba passed B.Sc. examination with very good results.

In the second year I traveled New Delhi and Mumbai once with my parents. These two are big cities. Do the cities show the actual picture of India? Thoughts came to me. Are these cities not covers up of the poverty of India?

Second year passed. I passed exam and promoted to third year. But Apu failed in second year. I met him in his house. I was not in touch with Aruba for some days. She told me when Apu went to his room,

'You have come to know, that Apu has failed in his exam. Why did he fail? I noticed for few months, he did not talk openly. I thought, due to burden of study he behaved that way. I think something wrong is going with Apu.'

Aruba was weeping. I was very sad seeing tears in her eyes. Last year I did not enquire about him for many days. I felt, it was my fault not to meet Apu frequently. I said to her, 'Please do not be much worried. I shall talk to Apu about the problems he faced.'

Apu and I came out. We walked on road for some time. Then we sat on a bench in the nearby park. I asked him to tell me about his problems and why he failed in exam. He replied, 'Even from the first year, I felt that I was in lack of my study. Anyhow I passed to second year. In second year I was weak internally. I could not concentrate in my study. You know, I suspected, someone fed me something related to drugs during ragging in hostel by some seniors!'

Hearing him I was frightened. I came to conclusion that some of the hostel- mates had made him habit of addiction to drugs. I returned home with him. Calling Aruba outside I told her, 'Apu's mental condition is not good. Tomorrow we have to take him to a psychiatrist without fail.'

Following day Aruba and I with Apu called on a specialist in psychiatry. After examining Apu the specialist told, 'You should have brought him before. Keep him at a distance from mental stress.

Medicines for one month have been prescribed. Come after a month.' When Aruba and Apu came out from the chamber, I told the doctor, 'We have suspicion on Apu of taking drugs. What type of treatment will be better to him?' The doctor replied, 'Feed the prescribed medicines for the month, then to examine him again.'

We reached home with Apu. We did not talk much on the way. I was angry with myself. Few months back Aruba one day told me, 'I suspect something has happened to Apu. At that time I did not pay much attention to her words. I should have told her to take Apu to a physician then. I thought then, there were many doctors and specialists in the medical college and Apu would take treatment easily, if he had any disease. Actually I was wrong. Worries and anxieties were seen on the faces of Apu's parents. I came to my home after telling Aruba to feed medicines regularly to Apu.

After two weeks the incident happened. No one could imagine. Apu swallowed all the medicines and sleeping tablets at night. He was taken to hospital in unconscious state in the morning. He was in dying condition. In the struggle for life and death, Apu died after two days. He departed to an unknown space.

I could not believe myself– death came to Apu! I could not face Aruba's grievous condition and could not find words to console her. How much painful the blow of the death! No one can feel except the near and dear ones.

Some days elapsed. Sometimes I came to Aruba's house. She is still mentally disturbed. She was in final year of M. Sc. She also wanted to appear in Assam Public Service Commission Exam (APSCE). But the death of Apu had come as a death-blow to her.

I said to Aruba, 'You have to face all the events courageously and try to sit in your examinations. If you become meek and weak, Apu's soul will not get peace.' Aruba only gazed at my face.

I could not take Apu's death at ease. I was suffering a lot mentally. Students of my class decided to go to educational excursion to New Delhi, Agra and some other places.

On the day before going for excursion I went to see Aruba. I said, 'My mind is at distress. My class-mates have arranged an excursion to New Delhi and other places. I think, change will give me some relief.'

She said, 'This time you go. Afterwards all of us will go for traveling.'

My classmates were in happy mood. We spent three days in New Delhi. Then we went to Agra. My class friends were very jolly to see the Tajmahal. But I was not happy. Thoughts came to me, 'Emperor Shahjahan built the Tajmahal on memory of his queen Mamtaj. Tajmahal is called a token of love. But the architect of the Tajmahal was murdered by the emperor. The emperor made the costly peacock throne. He spent lots of money in luxury. Nadir Shah looted the throne. Aurangzeb became emperor of India after he kept his father Shahjahan in jail. Result of expenditure in luxury and negligence in strong rule is the downfall.

Today most of our ministers, legislators and bureaucrats have collected wealth for luxury by backdoor policy. They will be jailed one day in the judgment of the God or of the people; time will tell. Blindness to love, wealth and luxury brings the downfall to the kings or the ruling power one day. It brings disasters to the people in the long run.

After two weeks we returned to Guwahati. I could not join heartily with my happy friends. Some unknown sign kept me away from enjoying joy and pleasure. I came to see Aruba the following day. We talked and discussed in some subjects.

This way my third year was about to end. Sometimes I met Aruba in her house. Aruba appeared in M. Sc. final exam. APSC exam was also over.

Aruba passed M. Sc. in first class. She also passed in APSC exam. She informed me regarding the date of oral exam in APSC.

I passed my third year examination and admitted in fourth year, that is final year. On the day after oral exam of Aruba, I came to enquire her about exam. She said that she had done well in examination. But I noticed, she said with a disappointment. After some conversation, she told me to meet her next day in the University canteen for some discussion. I thought, Aruba never told me to meet her outside. But this time suspicion came to my mind.

Next day in the afternoon I met her at the University canteen. But we sat on the bench outside the canteen. She asked me, 'Shall I get any benefit if I join in ULFA? Is it possible to get independence to Assam?'

I was surprised. I shouted, 'Joining in ULFA! What do you mean? Tell me the actual matter.'

Aruba said, 'Amit, you know, what happened yesterday in APSC oral examination! One member asked, 'Why do girls want government job? Better to get married.' Another one remarked, 'You are a beautiful girl.' Again another member said, 'Is it possible now-a-days to get a good job without a price?' I lost my temper. I shouted at them, 'Do you not know manners how to behave with a girl in the oral examination? Are you not ashamed of your uncultured manners? How much bribe did you paid to become member or chairman? And how much bribe have you taken from candidates till date?' After this I came out from the room. I know, I shall not get the job. Apu's death wounded me deeply. I imagined you as Apu and thinking about my parents, I got courage to sit in examinations. I thought, after getting a job I shall be busy in work and shall forget about the past.'

After hearing Aruba's words, I was stunned. Breaking the silence I said to her, 'You have done the right thing. You have given a fitting reply to the misdeeds of such people. They will not forget for their whole lives. They have got a lesson from you. You do not know how much money these corrupt people are paying to the ULFA. I would have also replied to them in very rude way.'

Aruba said, 'I feel relieved of the pain in speaking to you about the incident. It seems to be free to me.'

I said, 'Do not take the name of ULFA from today. ULFA is a dream of uncertainty. How many innocent people died at the hands of ULFA, police and army! Please leave the thought of seeking job, do the Ph.D. now.'

Aruba said, 'You have a reason. Truly we are passing days through an uncertainty.'

I felt the condition of her mind. After taking tea in the canteen I took her to her house. To me it came, Aruba was worried. Yesterday's incident had affected her badly. After the death of Apu, she had suffered from depression for some days. Thoughts frightened me of being Aruba depressed and disappointed again from the incident! I returned home with a damp mind.

After one week I met Aruba in her house. After talking for few minutes with her, I felt she talked absent mindedly. Anxiety increased in my mind. But I could not ask anything to Aruba. I made up my mind to take her myself to a doctor at the end of the week.

...After three days, the heart-rending incident happened. Aruba was hit by a bus and she died. She died due to disappointment and depression she suffered. It was a horror to me. Even knowing Aruba's state of mind, I did nothing for her. Apu died and now Aruba. I felt myself guilty for her death. Aruba left me after Apu. It could be difficult to me to live. It is not possible for me to stay here anymore. All inspirations for me to live had vanished.

After two days I said to my mother pretentiously, 'After so much study to take a degree is useless. After taking degree, we shall be fatigued running after jobs. Rather, it will be better to join ULFA and make Assam independent.'

I said these smilingly and my mother thought it as a fun. She said lightly,

'ULFA leaders are doing business in other countries and the rest are dying here. Rather, go to the Himalayas. You will meet there sages, pious and learned men. And gather knowledge and wisdom.'

All of a sudden I had got the trace of my path. The word 'Himalayas' in the mouth of my mother, bestowed me the clue of my life in future. I pondered,

'Mother, are you a goddess? you have shown my path, for which I offer my humble respect and devotion to you. Forgive me for my leaving and hurting you all.'

After two days, I left my home and college-hostel at Guwahati and boarded in a New Delhi-bound train. After staying for two days in New Delhi, I reached at Haridwar. I lodged in a temple-shrine. For free lodging and food, I was engaged for cleaning the floors of the temple daily. I performed ritual ceremony to the names of Apu and Aruba. I went Rishikesh and Dehradun once or twice. After staying for two months in the temple-shrine, I came to know many inner circles regarding management of the shrine. I was surprised to see the ways of living of some priests and some persons who came to stay in the shrine. All modern facilities of living with pleasure were available in the shrine guest-house rooms. They would feel uncomfortable without the air-conditioners. I thought to get rid of the shrine.

One day I came to Dehradun. I stayed in a *dharaImsala* of a shrine. Next day I was moving through the markets in Dehradun seeing the big shops. I was standing in front a big shop. Coming from inside, a man said to me, 'The owner of the shop Lalaji has called you.' I followed the man and entered inside. Lalaji (the businessman) asked me, 'Are you searching for something? You are waiting for some time at the front.'

I said, 'Nothing, I am actually searching for a job.'

Lalaji began to think for a while. Then he asked me whether I knew English and accounts-works. After a sharp thought, I replied in positive. He told me to come at 10 AM next day to meet him for discussion.

I arrived at 10 AM at Lalaji's shop following day. The shop was open.

Lalaji was also there. He asked me some questions. He appeared to be satisfied with my replies. I feared thinking that, Lalaji might suspect me being from Assam. I informed him factually. He understood that I was in need of money. After thinking for few minutes, Lalaji told me to join in my work from that very day. My work was to verify stocks, to write letters to the companies in English and to coordinate with Munimji (the accountant) in accounts works. When Lalaji asked me regarding salary I wanted, I said, 'You will pay my salary as you think me worthy.'

Lalaji had done another favour to me. In the backside of the shop there was a vacant room adjacent to the watchman's room. Lalaji told a man to clean the room. He told me to shift to the room next day leaving the *dharamsala* of temple. I thought, he understood my difficulties well.

I remained to stay at the room from the following day. Lalaji arranged my food in monthly basis in a nearby small hotel, for which he would pay.

Lalaji's shop was a big one dealing in hardware materials. More or less it could be called a company. There were big go-downs in other places.

Lalaji knew about the temple of the goddess Kamakhya at Guwahati, Assam. In the very first day he told me, 'I want to give you a new name. Kamakhya is a goddess, you cannot be named as Kamakhya. Here our god Kalkaji is famous. From today you are named 'Kalkaji'.' Other employees of the shop laughed. On Lalaji's wish, I was known as 'Kalkaji' to all from that day. Within one week, I learned many thing about the shop and its management.

After one month Lalaji took me to the Branch Manager of the nearby Bank to open a Bank account in my name. I had copies of my educational certificates and other documents with me. The Branch Manager cared much for Lalaji, as he dealt heavy amount of money with the Bank. Lalaji introduced me as the new assistant manager of his firm to the Branch manager. Smile came to me. Lalaji said to me, 'Your salary will be deposited in your bank account. Do not hesitate to ask for money from me for your urgent need.'

I did not think of money. My mind was moving in the thought of – after this where I should go and in which way! Apu and Aruba had left me. Their memory pained me always.

Lalaji read news paper daily. He made me to read also. Though I read Hindi newspapers, sometimes I brought English newspapers and read in my room. Sometimes I bought the Economics Times. I also discussed about the ups and downs of the price of goods. One day I told Lalaji, 'As per news paper report, the Price of iron materials may go up this time.' Lalaji thought for few minutes. He was an experienced business man. He had managed his business according to his choice. He told me, 'Let us sell iron goods in less quantity and keep stock more. It is a matter of one or two months only.'

Really, the price of iron materials was increased in the budget. Lalaji was happy to get more profit after the sale of goods. In the following month the employees were paid extra money in addition to their regular salaries. Lalaji told me in a low voice, 'Kalkaji, profit was more only for your advice. Your share of profit has been deposited in your bank account by Munimji as I told him.'

I smiled at Lalaji's words. I said,' I have done nothing. It is only your own decision.'

Lalaji said, 'There is risk always in business. It is a matter of heavy amount. Sometimes doubt comes. This time I got courage from you. Therefore, here is your hand this time.'

I noticed, though Lalaji was a businessman, he was kind and wise. He never behaved his employees rudely. Employees also regarded him. Slowly my faith and respect to Lalaji began to increase.

Lalaji sometimes took me to his home. His house was at two kilometer distance from the shop. In the first floor Lalaji and his family resided. Ground floor was rented. Members of Lalaji's family were his wife whom everyone called as Mataji (elder mother), his elder son Ravi, daughter -in-law, three year old grandson and his younger son Piku. Ravi had a big bicycle-shop at a little distance. Piku was studying in College.

Lalaji said to me, 'My elder son Ravi was not a good student in study. I have made him to do his own bi-cycle business. He was given in marriage too. I do not know what my younger son Piku will do! He is a commerce student and average in study. Our only daughter was married off some years back. She was married to a business family at Saharanpur.'

Some days back I purchased a transistor. I got ease from listening the transistor. I listened to news of the country and sometimes songs. Lalaji always came to shop at 10 pm. in an auto rickshaw. He went home at 8 pm. He travelled in the auto-rickshaw whenever he was to go outside. At noon he went home for lunch. Sometimes food for lunch for Lalaji were sent to the shop. One day I asked Lalaji, why he did not purchase a car. He said to me, 'To purchase a car is easy for me. I shall travel in the car and my sons will also ask for a car. To run the car a driver will be necessary. All in total will increase my head ache. Sons will be luxurious and idle. There is a motorbike for their use'. I found logic in Lalaji's words.

All the members of Lalaji's family called me Kalkaji. Mataji was a kind lady. They took me as a member of their family. Lalaji spent time at home with his grandson. Ravi and Piku were polite and courteous. The daughter-in-law also respected Lalaji and Mataji. One day Mataji asked me in presence of Lalaji, whether I remembered my home in Assam. Lalaji swiftly said, 'Every now and then, we get news of bursting of bombs and killing of innocent people by terrorists in Assam. Do not want to go to Assam in such dangerous time.' I thought, 'Lalaji has good faith in me as a good boy.'

When I was at Haridwar, I visited many temples there. I visited Ganga temple, Haricharan temple, Sakti peeth of the Sati and Blue hill. I also visited temples in Dilkesh hill – temple of goodess Manasha and Sapta sorovar spring and so on. Now at Dehradun I have seen – a town of natural beauty and comfortable climate. Dehra means rest – place and Dun means valley. Hence the famous name is Dehradun or Deradun. Here are many modern schools and colleges. Residential schools are in numbers. Boys and girls from all over the country come to study here in schools. There are Indian Military Academy, Forest Research Institute, Indian Petroleum Institute etc. There is the Braille Press to print books for the blind. The Military cantonment in Dehradun is a big one. There are degree Colleges and Post Graduate Colleges in Dehradun.

There is said that Lord Rama and Lakshmana after killing Ravana travelled to the pilgrimage of the Himalayas through this valley to be free from the sin of man-slaughter. In the same way five Pandavas after killing the Kauravas and others travelled to the Himalayas for pilgrimage to get liberty of the bondage of sins. There is Topovan nearby, where sage Dronacharya meditated. At fifteen kilometras away from Dehradun there is the place Sahashradhara. At Sahashradhara there are rivulets and spring of Sulphur. It is believed that taking a bath in the spring of Sulphur, heals all kinds of diseases. Sahashradhara is a beautiful place surrounded by hills. In the main market place in Dehradun, the clock tower place is a busy market area. From the park here, the scenery of hill station Mushouri is very charming to see. The scene of Mushouri at night from Dehradun becomes fascinating During winter season scenery of snow-bound Mushouri becomes wonderful. From Dehradun, distance to Mushouri is 35 kilometers, to Rishikesh 42 kilometers and to Haridwar 65 kilometers. Within hundred kilometers from Dehradun, there are Dakpathar, Chakrata and some other places of beautiful scenery. Journey through the zig- zag road from Dehradun to Mushouri gives pleasure to mind.

When I went outside Lalaji sent Piku with me. The development work of Dehradun and Mushouri were done by the British. The British occupied Dehradun from the Gurkhas. Mushouri was discovered by military officer Captain Young in 1827. At first Young constructed a holiday resort at Mushouri. Mushouri is called the "Queen of hills." Now – a – days Mushouri is a big tourist-place. Snow-covered scenes of Mushouri are enchanting in winter. Nearby Mossi falls and Camy falls are very nice places. There are residential schools and many hotels and guest houses in Mushouri.

Children of ministers, bureaucrats and rich business-men get chance in these residential schools. It is difficult to understand - the students of these costly schools have become leaders or highly placed officials without knowing the factual conditions of the people of India. In Assam, students leaders became ministers and legislators in AGP government. Some of them made a rush to send their children to the costly schools at Mushouri and Dehradun. But there were the leaders of AASU, who bought betel-nuts in credit from the vendors in the University campus, but forgot to pay. It is surprise! AGP leaders or Congress leaders, - all of them at first think of their own and families. Some of AASU and AGP leaders defected to Congress party. and became very rich and powerful. Not only in Assam, in the whole of India, the conditions are same. Seeing the mentality of present leaders in power, can the soul of Gandhiji who knew the inner pains of the poor people of India, do something for them?

In my room I kept some religious and science books. Listening to songs in the transistor, I read the books till midnight. One day, seeing the religious books in my room, Lalaji said to me, 'You are studying religion in such a young age, do you want to be a sage?' I only smiled.

Lalaji told me openly about his life. His early life was not so happy. His father died, after he studied in College for two years. With the family pension and rents from two small rooms, his mother maintained family with difficulties. He left college in the middle and did some small business. He made his younger brother well educated. Now his brother had constructed his own house at a distance of five kilometers from Lalaji's house. He had a good job in the Forest department. There was harmony between two brothers. Gradually Lalaji's business began to grow well and reached the present state. Calculations of the property tax, income tax and sales tax were done by a chartered accountant and taxes were deposited in time. In these matters Lalaji was very regular.

I remained busy in work in day time, thereby I tried to forget my painful thoughts. Different thoughts came to mind – 'How many days I would spend in this way! Sometimes I thought about Assam, my home. What did my parents think about me? They might think that I had joined in ULFA! Apu and Aruba are no more. But how their parents are now! What they are doing!' Worries and anxieties disturbed me. Associating with a man like Lalaji, I got courage to get rid of worries. From the experience of life, he got the strength to judge others. I thought, Lalaji perhaps loved me. He never asked me such questions which might hurt me.

Lalaji did not like the politicians. Political parties asked for donations. With reluctance he donated money. In anger Lalaji uttered, 'With the people's money, these leaders fight elections, capture power and spend days with comfort and pleasure.'

When I was alone in my room, these thoughts worried me – 'Polities of today are very much different from the polities of the past days. In the politics of yore, might have some doubts in competency but corruption was not there perhaps. To-day in the politics, competency may not prevail, but corruption remains there. And there have been now waves of politics in dynastic route for politicians. Political murders are happening from the yore. After the assassination of John F. Kennedy then President of the USA, horror of murder and death came to the family. Prime Minister of India, Mrs. Indira Gandhi was killed by her body guard. Being blind to religion, the body-guard killed her. Intelligence Agencies failed to verify even the body guard of the Prime Minister, then how would the agencies be successful in other important matters! Certainly, doubt remains. Killing of Indira Gandhi brought the curse of death to the family. Her son Rajib Gandhi, former primer Minister of India was the victim of killing. Her son Sanjoy Gandhi also died prematurely in accident. To save the Congress Party, Congress leaders brought Rajib Gandhi and his family. Would the fate of Gandhi family be like that of Kennedy family? Questions comes to my mind.

In 1962, at the Indo-China battle, China defeated India badly. In eastern India, after occupying upto

Bomdila, Chinese army returned. China made the Indian prisoners of war free. India took it granted that China would never attack again. India failed to know, why Chinese army left Bomdila after its occupation. The mystery of leaving Bomdila was – 'China has bigger plan for future against India. China says that it does not recognize Macmohan line, as border mark between the two. Friendship between Pakistan and China has raised suspicion to India. There is also doubt about the defence preparedness of India. Appointments of Commanders for war and defence depend on the wishes of the ministers and bureaucrats. Also, criteria are judged on the basis of states and languages.

Many times appointments are not done in merit basis and thereby displeasure arises among ranks. It is difficult to serve the country with displeasure and disappointment in mind. Result is inevitable – ill-effects. In all spheres, transparency should be maintained.'

'There is a practice in England, the crown-prince should get experience in all fields of the country. From cleaning cowshed to military-training, he gathers knowledge of experience. In India how many political leaders or bureaucrats gather knowledge of practical experience! No one can win a battle or know the soil of the land, sitting in highly decorated chambers in lofty buildings. In Indo- China battle, Indian solders had no proper weapons, did not get proper warm clothes and did not find proper food. But crores of rupees were spent by the defence ministry. Now India has sufficient weapons; but a major part of money goes to the middle men in defence deals. In purchases of provisions, big corruption prevails. Many corrupted leaders and bureaucrats have made our country crippled. They have no patriotism. They have nepotism and favoritism, they have weak leadership and incompetency. They are self- interested. There are only small number of honest and competent leaders and bureaucrats in the country China occupied Tibet. Indian government offered shelter to the Dalai Lama and many Tibetan refugees. India showed magnanimity. What did India do other than that? India voiced in the U.N.O. against the annexation of Tibet by China. But now India is silent.

Kailash-Manash-Sarovar lake is the holiest place for the Indians. From the immemorial time, the Kailash-Manash-sarovar has been associated with Indian philosophy and religion. It is also associated with the age of the Ramayana and the Mahabharata. Let the period of subjugation of India leave; Indian leaders after getting power in independent India, had forgotten the glory of past Indian civilization. Had the Indian leaders thought, today Kailash-Manash-Sorovar would have been in Indian map. But they did not get time to think about, being in power even. Today for pilgrimage to the Kailash Manash Sorovar, permission of Chinese authority is necessary. What a ridicule of history! But the leaders and bureaucrats of independent India do not forget to build costly rest houses for their own use in the summer season in Dehradun and Mushouri. This is the credibility of the majority of Indian leaders and bureaucrats! If China could annex Tibet, then why India could not occupy Kailash-Manash-Sarovar? Many questions arose to me.

One Sunday Lalaji took me to his younger brother's home. He told me earlier that lunch would be served there. Lalaji and others in his family are vegetarians. They like bread (*roti*), ghee, pulses and vegetables. They prefer bread to rice. But I prefer rice. During the first three months I ate fish in hotel sometimes. After that I also became a vegetarian totally. But rice remained more preferable to me than bread. Lalaji and myself reached at his brother's house. They began to talk. His brother felt discomfort to talk freely with Lalaji in my presence. Lalaji then said to him,' You have met Kalkaji before. Don't worry, you can speak freely.' Members of family of Lalaji's brother were – his wife, son Jintu and daughter Shravana. Jintu works in a office at Dehradun. Talks were going on marriage of Jintu. But parents were willing to get their son married after the marriage of their daughter. I came to know from their conversation that their problem was with the daughter Shravana.

Shravana that year was studying in the 1st year M.A. in Philosophy. She was in love with a youth who worked in a office at Dehradun. The youth was from lower caste. Therefore, the parents were not willing to get her married to the youth in any way. Their daughter also had said that she would not marry other than the youth. Shravana and her mother brought tea and sweets for us. Lalaji introduced me to them. Both the brothers' opinion was same – 'This marriage cannot be permitted. The society will laugh at us'. The brother told Lalaji that Shravana was informed many times in this regard but she was adamant. After taking tea I sat on the bench in veranda. I was enjoining the scene outside reading a news paper.

After some time we took meal. Lalaji already told them that I liked rice. After taking rest for one hour, Lalaji and myself left the house. We were in an autorickshaw. Lalaji said that his brother was much worried with his daughter. I said, 'In our Assam, marriages among upper and lower castes are normal matter. Our society is not so much conservative. Your society is very conservative regarding marriage. In your place the family of the bridegroom demand much dowry from the family of the bride. In our places, there is no custom of dowry.'

Lalaji said, 'There is the demand of dowry. The marriages among upper and lower castes in our places, are taken as an insult. Therefore, the family is suffering a not.'

I said, 'If the youth actually loves her, they can get married in the court.' Lalaji said, 'Your opinion is good. But there is also difficulty if the youth or his family do not agree. All right, I shall call mother and daughter on telephone tomorrow. I shall ask the daughter openly regarding the opinion of the youth or his family.'

Shravana was two or three years younger to me. There was rush of youths to marry her, but the family had to refuse the good proposals due to daughter's love for the youth.

Following day afternoon, Mataji informed Lalaji on telephone that Shravana and her mother had come to house. Lalaji asked me to go with him. I thought, Lalaji perhaps called them as he said yesterday.

Both of us entered the drawing room. Shravana greeted Lalaji touching his feet. She also greeted me calling 'Hallo, Kalkaji.' I greeted Mataji, Shravana and her mother whom I called Aunty. Lalaji wanted to take tea first. He asked Mataji to bring some eatables along with tea. Mataji returned to the room calling her daughter-in-law to make tea. Lalaji went to bathroom. Mataji chatted with us. Lalaji returned to the room. Tea and eatables were brought by the daughter-in- law. After taking tea I wanted to go out side. But Lalaji asked me to remain there. Lalaji began to speak, 'Shravana, I want to discuss with you some important matter. Do not fight shy, tell us openly. We cannot get you married to the youth socially. If you want, there is a way. Court-marriage may be done. Do you know something about the opinion of the youth and his family?'

Embarrassed Shravana replied, 'I discussed but the boy wanted the marriage to be performed socially. I may ask him again, but do not hope he will agree.'

I had listened to them silently. Suddenly Lalaji asked me, 'Kalkaji, can you tell me, why the boy is refusing court-marriage?' I tried to find words to reply. After a pause I said, 'In our state if guardians do not permit lovers to get married, the lovers go to some temple to get married or in the court, marriage is registered. The boy, in this case, has urged for social marriage. To me, the boy probably has thought of deprivation of dowry if the marriage is registered in court. The boy might have greed for dowry. Of course, now everything depends on Shravanaji and the boy. But I may be wrong in my views.'

Silence remained for few moments. Lalaji said, 'Your observations are good. But I cannot find a way how to solve the main problem. Shravana, final decision depends on you.'

I said, 'All of you are worried about the marriage of Shravanaji. A uncertainty prevails. I think it will be better to Shravanji to continue study to get the M.A. degree. In between a solution will come.'

Mataji and Aunty also said that Shravana herself should think of future course. Lalaji said, 'For the time being, it will be a relief, but I do not know what will happen in coming days. Shravana, let us know a little what is in your mind.'

With face downcast Shravana was listening. With a thoughtful mind she said, 'At present I want to get rid of marriage, I want to complete my M.A. degree.'

Lalaji said, 'All right, tell your father openly. I myself shall also talk.

Thereafter, Shravana and her mother went to their home. Lalaji remained at his home. I had to take dinner with him as he wanted.

After entering my room, many thoughts came to me. So many incidents happen in the life of man! I wanted to recollect the happenings of the day – Sometimes peculiar situations arrive in the families! What is present actual situation in Assam? I looked at the leaves of my diary. Sometimes I wrote in the diary. My eyes stopped at a leaf. I began to read – 'Murders are going on at many places in Assam. Secret killings, political murders and murders for selfish motives are happening. Extreme miseries have come to the affected families. No investigations, no trial and no punishment are applicable against the culprits. Not only in Assam, all over India, how many deaths of innocent people have occurred! Those in powr do not want to punish the guilty on political reasons. In 1984 a Sikh body guard killed Indira Gandhi. After the incident, about three thousand Sikhs were killed by the Congress men. They were burnt to death, houses were torched. No trial had been done till date. The guilty are not punished on politically motivated reasons. The Sikhs also began to forget the calamity in political grounds!

As I was drowsy I slept. In morning seeing my diary on the table, I kept it inside my bag so that others cannot see it. There were many personal writings in the diary.

After two weeks, one day Lalaji fed sweets to others in the shop. For, Piku passed B.Com. Result is not so satisfactory, but at least he passed. Lalaji was happy – Piku is now a commerce graduate. Lalaji took me home with him. There, I met Shravana and her mother. They had come to enquire the result of Piku. With a greeting to them, I sat on chair in the room. I noticed, Shravana was talking comfortably now. Lalaji took his seat near me. Shravana said, 'Uncle is now relieved of an anxiety. Piku will help uncle a little in business now onwards.' Piku who was sitting beside, smiled.

I said, 'Lalaji is now grey headed. So, Piku not a little but wholly is to take responsibility from him. Lalaji should take rest henceforth.'

Lalaji told me, 'You have said the right thing. Piku's pass in examination has relieved me a lot. But he is weak in English and other subjects. From now onwards you take care of Piku in learning of all matters.

We took sweets in good atmosphere. I thought of Shravana to ask regarding her marriage and study. After a second thought, I did not. All were in jolly mood at the home. Addressing them I became ready to go to my room. Piku offered a lift to me on the bike.

It was Sunday. The shop was closed. I got a move in the town. There are Garwali People at large numbers at Dehradun. But they have no big business in their hands. Punjabis, Marowaries and other people have business houses. There are Hindus and Christians. During the partition of India, some Bengali families of refugees were placed here. I talked less to the people I met in the town. For, I had suspected, somebody might know me. Now I could speak Hindi fluently. Lalaji's family members might not think that I was from a non-Hindi speaking state. There are big book-shops here. In the shops I got a glance on books. I purchased some books if chosen. Sometimes I went to the libraries also. I read news papers and magazines hurriedly. From the rail station many long distance trains run from here. This is the end point of incoming trains.

It came to my mind – 'The paths of Gandhiji and Netaji were different. Gandhiji's path was non-violent, but thousands of people died at the hands of the British. Azad Hind Fauz was made under the leadership of Netaji with the help of Military force of Japan, to fight against the British. Many deaths came. In the name of non-violence and military revolt, so many Indians lost their lives. At 'the divide and rule' Policy of the British, India had to pay the extreme price – the partition of India and horrible repercussion. Death of Netaji is still a mystery. Congress leaders had a fear – if Netaji would appear living, leadership of the nation could have gone to hands of Netaji. Commission after Commission was formed, but the truth of missing of Netaji still was not revealed. The mystery remains alive till today.'

I was in the shop. Piku arrived after a while. He passed B.Com in Hindi medium. I gave him my two books on store keeping and accountancy to study at his home. He said to me, 'Father will not come today. He has been feeling unwell. Though he has a bit high blood pressure, he takes tablet sometimes.' Munimji deposited cash and cheques of previous day in bank. Munimji is an experienced man. He maintained cash book efficiently. At the end of the month I took out a statement of profit and loss. For payments, Lalaji signed in cheques. On the 2nd or 3rd day of the months, salaries of the employees were paid. Muninji deposited my salary in my Bank account.

After the closing time of the shop I went to see Lalaji with Piku. Lalaji was reading a Hindi news paper. He said to me, 'Nothing is to be worried. Sometimes pressure comes high.' I said, 'It will be better to examine once by a doctor. At least the anxiety will go.'

Next day Lalaji was examined by a doctor. After examination the doctor said,' Don't worry. Take ghee less and take more fruits.'

One year passed for me at Dehradun. I spent one year after coming from the temple at Haridwar. I thought, 'After this where I shall go! What I shall do!'. It was a deep relationship between Lalaji and myself. He had good faith on me. And in the same way, I had high respects for him. A good quantity of money was in my bank account. If I wished I could go to other place. Sometimes I thought about moving in places in the Himalayas. It was not possible for me to return to my home.

Recently I purchased a copy of the Bhagavat Geeta, the religious book. I had read some chapters. So many things are in the Geeta to learn. In Sanskrit verse- 'Karmonyodhikaraste, Ma Phalesu Kadason'- that means, there is 'a right to work, but never in the result.' We should not be worried for the result. In the battle field our duty is to fight, it is not the time to think of the outcome. There is in the Geeta – 'To abstain from the clutches of the senses, is the proper accomplishments of Yoga, the religious practice. Closing the doors of the body in the forms of senses, keeping the mind in the heart and fixing the vital breath on top point of the head, one can get super natural position.' Again there is written – 'Those whose minds are addicted to unspoken, similar forms of supreme being, for them it is difficult to get spiritual salvation. To proceed in this way for corporeal bodies, is more difficult always.'... To win is the motto in war. Common people should go on working in the general state. But for all same result may not come. After hard work some do not get expected outcome, but some others may get easily. Perhaps, people called it destiny. But having faith in destiny and without working, to expect something is unwise.

After getting the news that Shravana had passed M.A. First year exam., Piku and myself went to her house. Conversation went on in good environment. Sweets were served to us. I was surprised when Shravana asked me,' Kalkaji, why did you leave Engineering College without taking degree?' I felt pain to reply. I said,' After getting the degree in engineering, of course I would get good employment. And I would marry a girl with a big dowry.' All began to laugh hearing me.

Shravana said,' In your place there is no custom of dowry. Therefore, to get dowry the girl should have been from North or South India.

Again all laughed loudly. I said,' Then, please leave the chapter of marriage. Now after moving here and there, I wish to go to the Himalayas one day. Shravanaji, how did you know me about those things?'

Shravana replied,' I came to know from Mataji.'

I said,' Different things are discussed with Lalaji. Probably, Lalaji told Mataji about me.'

Aunty said,' I have only heard of the Himalayas now-a-days on the mouth of a boy like you. You have years to go to the Himalayas.'

Shravana said, 'Kalkaji, on the principle of Philosophy, you have spoken of pessimism. Some one in life can suffer from pessimism for a period. But that may not be permanent. One incident creates another one, and that may be better one.'

I said,' Shravanaji, has the Himalayas not influenced effective optimism than pessimism for ages? In the past the great wise sages living in the Himalayas, created the ever lasting treasures of knowledge. I have only a small wish to know something about the spiritual culture of India.'

Before Shravana said something, her father told,' Now, both of you conclude your debate. Do you want to come to the end of the debate today itself?'

Again all laughed. Piku and I took leave of them. Piku dropped me in my room.

Condition of Lalaji's health was better now. He used to come to shop. Piku and myself decided regarding supply orders. Of course, Lalaji's voice was final. Though Lalaji came to shop, he only remained for two or three hours.

Soemtimes Lalaji called me to his house. He was thinking to build the second floor of the house. He said,' I want to build the second floor for boys for future. I have doubt about them in managing business in future. I have no much confidence on Rabi and Piku. They are not so much intelligent. In business, one needs courage and intelligence,'

I said,' Rabi is managing his business well. Piku also is learning well. Please do not take much tension on your head.'

Lalaji said,' I have full confidence on you. You can make Piku efficient in all spheres, suppose, you are my consultant or an adviser.' I said,' Your best adviser is Mataji.'

He said,' She is the shareholder already. Do you not know now-a-days, about business management? So many young managers are managing big business houses efficiently. Age is not a barrier in merit.'

Mataji brought tea for us. She said to Lalaji,' You have spoken to Kalkaji as like he has appeared for an interview for service before you.' Lalaji and myself only smiled.

Lalaji said to me, 'Listen, no one knows what would happen in life. Therefore it is necessary to all to remain alert. Do not think, that danger would not come. The wise always remain alert against danger. There is always uncertainty in business. So, patience, courage and intelligence are necessary. If you do not get payment after supplying materials in time, what difficulties may arise – guess before hand about inconveniences you would face. Good men and bad men are there, and would remain so. If you have honesty and self- confidence, others will show respect to you. My idea is that, my sons are not matured enough. I have seen all virtues in you. You have great prosperity in future. Make Piku also efficient. He is not so keen that he will learn on his own. I am now aged. You are here, therefore, I am not much worried.'

After taking dinner with Lalaji I reached my room. I switched on the transistor. I feel comfortable in listening to music and songs of Lata Mangeshkar, the great singer. In Assam, I listened to the songs and music of singer Dr. Bhupen Hazarika. Tone of voice of songs of Dr. Hajarika seems to come from the depth of the heart. What ever as a man, but as an artiste and singer he is on high esteem. In the same way Lata Mangeshkar's voice touches the hearts of listeners. From the transistor, I got some conveniences- listening to news of the country and listening to old Hindi songs. Songs gave me at least some comfort in my mind. Piku witnessed cricket play in television. He called me also. But I was not interested to witness play. It was waste of time and a bad habit – I thought. Lalaji listened news but was not interested in other programme in television. Mataji and the daughter-in-law witnessed religious serials.

Lalaji was busy in the next months. Construction work of the second floor was started. Roof-work was completed. Brick-work was to be started after few days. Lalaji showed me and consulted about the plan. He attended in shop for some days only and left early.

One day Lalaji called me to the home saying there was an important work with me. He took me to his bedroom. We talked for some time regarding shop and other matters. He asked Mataji to bring two empty glasses and a jug with water. To my surprise, Lalaji put a bottle of whisky on table.

He said to me, 'Today I want you to drink whisky with me. To drink alone, it is not comfortable.'

— 'I am coming to know that you do not drink all these.'

— 'Doctor has prescribed me to drink occasionally on health ground.'

— 'To me it is not like that you are to drink on health ground. Doctors themselves advise – 'take an apple a day and get free from all diseases.'

— 'Now-a-days, the young have a fashion to drink whisky, brandy. So, I do not mind if you drink a little with me. Rather, I have called you to give me company.

— 'No, no, I do not take all these things. I can sit with you but do not drink at all.'

He was about to open the whisky-bottle and said to me, 'You must drink a little at least. I open the bottle,'

I again said, 'If you open the bottle, you are to drink. I say truly, I do not touch wine or other intoxicating drugs.'

Lalaji gazed at my face. Then he called Mataji and asked her to take away glasses and the jug of water. He had kept the whisky-bottle inside the almirah. Then he said to me smilingly, 'You have spoiled my entertainment today.' Then we came out of the room and sat in the drawing room. Mataji brought tea for us. Lalaji listened news in T.V. For few minutes I also listened and then left.

Before going to my room, I took meal at the hotel. I had been taking meal in the hotel for more than one year. Rice, bread, curries of lentils and vegetables, ghee and butter were available in the hotel. Till now Lalaji had been paying my food-expense for every month.

After entering my room, many thoughts gathered in my mind. I wanted to recollect the happenings of the day. Lalaji wanted me to drink whisky. I refused him and felt peace in my mind for my refusal. But I had suspected, what Lalaji would think of me!

Lalaji did not come to shop following day. I felt relieved for his not coming. I would have hesitated before him for the incident happened in last night. Large quantity of materials arrived in godown day before. Piku and myself went to godown to check the materials. Two watchmen in the godown were very faithful and honest. Some materials were lying out side. Due to shortage of labourers all materials could not be stored inside. Labourers were engaged in morning. Both Piku and myself checked the materials. We checked up stock registers, copies of challans and invoices were checked. I came to the go- down before also. Piku had begun to come now. Salaries of the watchmen had been paid there. After two hours, we returned to shop.

After one week, I was in my room. Suddenly Piku arrived at my room riding the motor-bike. He said, 'Kalkaji, let us go immediately. Father is wounded after falling in bathroom.' Without delay, we reached home. After reaching I found, Rabi had made arrangement to take Lalaji in a taxi to hospital. Lalaji was talking weakly. Seeing me, he told me to remain beside him. Lalaji was taken to hospital and admitted there. After examining him by doctors, he was transferred to a cabin in the hospital. He was hurt on his head. There was probability of internal damage. Other tests had been done. His right hand was also wounded. It was difficult to lift the hand. Lalaji had to remain for a week in hospital. His relatives had visited him during the week. His daughter came to visit from Saharanpur. Shravana, her parents and her brother Jintu also often visited Lalaji in hospital. Other people known to Lalaji visited him. After one week, Lalaji was discharged from hospital. There was anxiety to all in the week. After discharge, he was taken home and all of us felt relieved. He was very weak. Lalaji could not sign in cheques. Lalaji and Mataji had joint bank accounts.

Mataji signed in cheques these days. She had always in anxiety regarding Lalaji's health condition. An early recovery would please all.

After one month Lalaji recovered fully. He attended shop two or three days for some time. He had asked me and Piku to take responsibilities. Piku had learnt much now.

One Sunday Piku and myself entered the house of Shravana on the way after visiting Sahashradhara. Shravana and her mother were at home. Talks were going on about marriage of Jintu. Bride was not finalized but talks with a family at Mujafornagar were in final stage. I thought to ask but stopped, after a second thought. I thought to ask her regarding her marriage.

Shravana said, 'Kalkaji, had you thought to ask something? Is it about my marriage?'

I was embarrassed at her question. I said, 'As you have expressed, tell a little about your marriage. Has anything progressed?'

She said, 'No progress, I have made up my mind. Perhaps I will not be married in my life.'

I said, 'Shravanaji, marriage may not come to one who wishes, but may come without one's wish. Therefore, let the marriage remain for future.' Aunty said, 'Both of you are addressing 'Ji' in your names. Differences of your ages will be hardly two or three years. It will be better for you to call by your names only.'

I wanted to avoid the topic of marriage of Shravana. I said to Aunti, 'Like your 'Ji', in our language also suffix 'deu' is added to show respect to someone. For example, 'touji' (father's elder brother) in Hindi will be ''jethadeu' in our language and 'taiji' will be called 'jethideu'.

Shravana said, 'Kalka is the name of a god, so suffix 'ji' must be added. All the more, Tauji had given the name to you.'

I said, 'Shravana is the name of a star, above the gods. So I should add 'ji' in your name.'

She said, 'I shall not match to debate with you. Let me bring tea for you.'

She went to kitchen.

Aunty talked to us. She enquired about the health of Lalaji.

Shravana brought tea and eatables. She asked me, 'Kalkaji, do you listen Hindi songs?'

I said,' Sometimes I listen Lata Mangeskar's songs.'

She said,' Then let us listen an old song of Lataji.' She had inserted the cassette of the Hindi Cinema 'Aap ki kasam' to play. I was enjoying the song 'Karvate badalte rahe – (changing the sleeping position of the body) single mindedly. I liked the song very much. Voices of Lata Mangeskar and Kumar Kishore and Music by R.D. Barman, had special attraction to me. I enjoyed the song reclining my head on sofa set with comfort. Truly, the melody of songs seemed to come from the inner side of heart of the singers. The songs of five minutes each duration seemed to end early for me though. I was sitting silently keeping eyes closed.

Hearing Shravana's voice I had waked up. Closing the cassette player she asked me, 'How do you feel listening the songs?'

I replied, 'Nice songs, specially the Karbaten Badalte Rahe.' She said, 'Shall I play the song again?'

I said, 'Today let it be stopped here. Afterwards one day I shall come to listen again,' Thereafter, Piku and myself left Shravana's house riding on the bike. Piku made me get down at my room.

After washing my hands and face, I came outside. The lighted town of Dehradun is very beautiful to see at night. After taking meal at the hotel I returned to my room. At my room I opened my diary. About two months passed, I had not written anything in my diary. I was in confusion due to Lalaji's sickness.

Taking the pen I began to write – 'I should not have been so reflective listening to the song of the 'Aap ki kasam' film at Shravana's house. What she would think about me! Actually the music and melody of the songs touched the heart.

Though I know Lalaji is a relieved person and healthy now, still I have apprehension about him. I know, if anything happens to Lalaji, I have to leave here. I have been here for his love and faith on me. I had lost Apu and Aruba. I know, due to my a little carelessness, I am also guilty for their deaths. I have not come out of guilt-feeling for their deaths. Here I have forgotten many things after meeting Lalaji and his members of family. There may be different languages and cultures amongst people. But the language of mind is the same for all. Hopes and problems of people are same. People want a home, a society without problems. Here I have noticed – People are not unhappy, have no useless anxiety. I do not know, what had happened to the people of Assam now! Where there is no surety of lives, how, smile would come to the faces of the people! Here people laugh openly, no question of cheating in work. They offer help to others in need. They do not talk much unnecessarily. Seeing military exercises in the beautiful grounds, it seems to me that all people here are protected. Hundreds of military trucks pass through the roads at a time. The scene is spectacular and delightful.

There is a road side shop of *'chingra'* (a kind of stuffed snack) and *'jelepi'* (a kind of sweet meat). Long queue of customers is seen for buying *'chingra'* and *'jelepi'*. They wait silently in the queue. Sometimes they wait for one hour or more. From distant places also customers come to the shop. Lalaji sends someone to buy *'chingra'* and *'jelepi'* sometimes. Those are eaten in shop and sometimes he takes *'chingra'* and *'jelepi'* to his home in the evening.

I would have been happy in Shravana's marriage to someone during my staying here. At least I could know her court-marriage or social marriage! Dowry system in marriage here, I can't take with ease. Parents suffer fear in the thought of getting married off their daughters. Indeed, the governments should emphasize in the education for woman, so that, women can be engaged in governmental establishment or self establishments. Being independent the unmarried girls may get relief of sufferings from fear of dowry in marriage. I feel sad when I think about caste - system in society here. Besides marriages, there are bad politics of castes here. In elections, people vote primarily for the candidates of their own castes, than the merits of the candidates here. Even being forward in education, people's mindset have not changed. People in Assam do not bother about someone's caste at least. In field of marriage, now- a-days Assamese society are free from conservatism. In election also influence of caste-system matters very little only. But the governments play politics with the linguistic and religious minorities.'

I felt sleepy. Keeping the diary carefully I went to bed.

Next day Lalaji called me to his home. Lalaji and other members were at home. I was sitting for some time, then Lalaji said, 'Kalakaji, tell the advantages after taking a car.'

Thought came to my mind, that Lalaji wanted to purchase a car. I said to him, 'You know better than me regarding advantages and disadvantages of a car. Yet I say, having your own car, you can go and move at your will, with your members of family. You can travel to other places comfortably. A car is essential for urgent and emergent matters. There is another advantage also – you can carry small articles and things. In this matter, the Ambassador car will be helpful. You can travel with members of your whole family with comfort.'

Lalaji said, 'You have cited regarding advantages, now tell me about disadvantage.'

I said, 'After purchasing the car, a driver will be necessary. You are to pay salary to the driver, spend for fuel, expenditure for repairing. To keep the car, a garage is necessary. You may get relief of a driver, if Rabi or Piku can drive the car.'

Mataji said, 'It will not be bad to purchase a car. When you were in hospital, lot of money had to be spent for Taxi and Auto fare.' Lalaji asked me, 'Can you drive a car?'

I said, 'I learned, can drive a car, but I have no driving licence' Lalaji asked, 'How many days will it take, if Piku learns to drive?'

I said, 'Learning time to drive varies for man to man. Some may learn well in a month. But some persons with fear in mind can't learn driving even with much efforts. Theoretically it seems easy to learn driving, but practically it is much different. For learning stage or afterwards a driver should be careful always keeping his or her two eyes, two feet and two ears always alert.'

Lalaji asked me about the brand of car, which would be helpful for them. I said, 'I have already told you that an Ambassador car will be much helpful for you and your family. There are many brands of cars in market, for pleasure driving. But I know, you want a car, which will be useful for you, not for pleasure.

Diesel fuel version of cars will cost more than Petrol version. But Petrol version cars are easy to maintain.'

After a week, a white colour Ambassador car was purchased by Lalaji. A driver drove the car home with Lalaji, me and Piku. A driver was engaged for some days.

Lalaji said, 'Let the driver be kept for few months, you know how to drive.

Piku will learn to drive, you will be with him.'

Learning of driving a car by Piku began. On Sundays the driver did not come. Piku and myself drove the car in college play-ground nearby. I tried to make Piku learn driving soon. On efforts of the driver and me, Piku learnt much within fifteen days. After one month Piku could take the car to drive on road in the driver's presence only. For, Piku and I had no driving licence.

To get a driving licence for me Lalaji first helped me to make an affidavit from court through a lawyer. Piku and myself submitted applications for driving licence with photos and other documents in the office of District Transport Officer.

After few days. Piku and myself were called for driving test by D.T.O. office. Piku, the driver and myself arrived with the car in the Office. The officer who tested our driving was sympathetic to us. He advised us not to drive with fear and carelessly. The officer was satisfied with our driving.

After few days both Piku and I got driving licence. Piku was very happy to get the licence. But I was different to get it. A driving licence could not be a matter of pleasure for me.

After a week, we visited Rishikesh and Haridwar in the car. Lalaji, Mataji, their daughter-in-law, grandson, Piku and myself were in the car. Most of time I drove. Piku also drove. We visited the temples and 'ashrams' in Rishikesh and Hardwar. I was happy for not visiting the temple, where I stayed in Haridwar.

In the next month, one day Lalaji, Piku and I went to visit Lalaji's married daughter's house at Saharanpur. We returned home late evening. After two days we were ready to visit hill queen Mushouri in morning. They had visited Mushouri some times before. This time the visit was with their own car. From the house Lalaji, Mataji, Piku and I started. In the way Shravana and her mother were taken in the car. Lalaji told me to drive. I was in discomfort with presence of Shravana in the car. It was difficult to openly talk when a girl was companion in the journey. Dehradun-Mushouri road is a hilly zigzag one with trees and beautiful scenery. We wore warm clothes. Snow-fall was going on in Mushouri. It was cold weather. Shravana and Piku took cameras with them. I tried to avoid camera from photographing with them. Yet they took some snap-shots with me. Snow-covered Moushouri is a charmful and wonderful place. I talked less with Shravana.

There are many clubs in Mushouri. Big shops and hotels are in Mall road. There are some churches. The British built the Mushouri town. It is one of the finest hill stations in India. The Danhill ropeway is very attractive to tourists. We visited Gandhi Chowk, Library bazaar and Clock Tower. The Christ Church is the oldest church. There are Castle hill estate, Survey of India Office, I.A.S. academy and Municipal gardens. Laltibba is the highest place in Mushouri. There is the military base in Laltibba. There are Tibetan Buddhist temple, Tibetan Schools and boarding houses. Happy valley area, Clouds End places are very nice to see. There are some water falls in and around Mushouri. There are some similarities of Mushouri with our Shillong. Mushouri is cleaner than Shillong. Snow-falling scene at Mushouri is a most pleasurable sight.

We took lunch at a restaurant. Lalaji, Mataji and Aunty made the situation very loveable and interesting with their talks. Lalaji said, 'The British built Dehradun and Mushouri and kept the towns very clean. They always maintained cleanliness. Now we the Indians, do not know to keep clean. We have no earnestness for the country amongst us.' We were a bit tired of moving around.

Lalaji said to me,' Being a young man, you should not be tired so soon.

Will you be able to drive?'

I said, 'Piku is there. He also now can drive well. There will be no problem.'

He said, 'No, no, Piku should not drive today. One day Piku and you come to Mushouri. Piku will drive, you will be with him. Then only his actual training will be over.' All of us enjoyed amusement at Lalaji words.

Shravana said, 'We feel tired. Let us take a cup of coffee each, we will feel comfort.'

Entering a coffee shop, we took coffee. Evening began to fall. As per Lalaji's wish we return to the car, so that we could return to Dehradun before darkness fell. We started for our return journey. On the way Lalaji, Mataji and Aunty were talking. Shravana, Piku and myself were silent. Lalaji told how he came to Mushouri on foot with some friends in boyhood days from Dehradun. From Mushouri the scene of lighted Dehradun is beautiful.

We reached Dehradun in less than one hour. Shravana and Aunty got down in front of their house. I stopped the car in front of the shop and got down. Piku drove the car with Lalaji and Mataji to their home.

Entering my room I washed hands, face and feet. I was tired of moving around and driving for the day. I took a cup of tea in a nearby shop. I walked for a while on the main road. I returned to the hotel and took a little meal and returned to my room.

Sitting in my room, I began to recollect the day's journey to Mushouri. I spent the day with all of them in good spirit. Their faces were amusing. I asked

Shravana, 'You had certainly come to Mushouri before one or more times. How do you feel this time about Mushouri?' In reply she said.' I came to Mushouri in school days. Then it was different. I came after, many times. Now moving around Mushouri, I have been thoroughly immersed. Actually, development of experience depends on age, state of mind and situation.' I said, 'Truly, state of mind prevails upon understanding of atmosphere. I have gathered today a lot of experience moving around the environment of Mushouri with you. Natural scenery of Mushouri is surely a dream land. 'She said, 'Every time I come to Mushouri, it seems to me new one. 'Lalaji said, 'Now-a-days number of tourists to Mushouri has been increasing every year. But the authority does not give attention for keeping the town beautiful and clean.' Tiredness of the day made me go to sleep.

One week after, on Sunday Lalaji went to visit Sahashradhara. Piku and myself went to Sahashradhara many times. I told Lalaji to take Piku to drive.

Piku had to drive car onwards from now. I wanted to take rest for that day and read books. On afternoon I went to railway station. I spent some time in the railway station. I read the time - table. Then I came to bus station. Read the time- table there. After moving around for some time I came back to my room. Sitting in room I thought – 'Lalaji could have purchased a car before. No shortage of money is for him. His business is going well. I have noticed, people here purchase a car for necessity, not for pleasure. In our Assam many people purchase cars for pleasure, not for necessity. There is an unannounced competition amongst them, who can purchase more costly cars, specially amongst them who earn money with corruption and unethical ways. Here I have seen cars are driven obeying traffic rules. In Assam, specially in Guwahati many car and motor bike drivers break the traffic rules. Traffic Police also remain as silent spectators. In many cars, number - plates are written in such way that it is difficult to read them. What ever styles they want, they write in those ways. There is no time to check them by Traffic Police or District Transport Office. It is difficult to catch those cars whenever any accident is done and speedily run away even killing someone. Police also pretend not to see them. Police are afraid to fine or punish the wrong doers, because they fear the rule- breakers may be sons or brothers-in-law of ministers, M.L.As., police officers or highly placed bureaucrats. What the present condition of Assam is! I feel hurt thinking about. I went to the hotel and returned after taking meal.'

After the month one day Lalaji suffered from heart-stroke. All were busy running after hospital and home. After struggling for three days between life and death, Lalaji breathed his last. He could not be saved in spite of all efforts by doctors.

A shadow of darkness came to the family members. An anxiety of fear was seen on their faces.

They cried and cried. I wept silently. Ravi performed all religious rites. He applied fire to the face of Lalaji's dead body at cremation. Lalaji's mortal body disappeared and merged with five elements as per faith of Hindu religion.

During the days when Lalaji was in hospital, his relatives flocked to enquire his health. Now everywhere there was silence. Death of Lalaji made all of us helpless.

I was also busy with others in death ceremony of Lalaji's departed soul. I was forced to forget other things. A solitary and silent atmosphere was prevailing in the surroundings. The bazar was closed for one day for mourning the death of Lalaji. The shop remained closed for one week. After opening the shop there was only silence. A thought of sadness was on all of us.

It passed more than one month. Piku remained in shop for most of time. Mataji came sometimes. She called me often to her home. She enquired from me whether Piku would be able to run the shop efficiently. I assured her not to be worried about Piku. She said to me, 'Kalkaji, you make Piku learn everything like you. You know well how Lalaji managed the business properly. Therefore, take the full responsibility with Piku to run the business efficiently.'

I said,' Lalaji kept Ravi in his bi-cycle business. I think henceforth, Ravi and Piku take the responsibility of the hardware shop also.'

Mataji said,' Lalaji wanted Ravi to concentrate in his own business. Piku and you take the charge of Lalaji's business from now onwards. There may be differences and misunderstandings between two brothers in doing business together. Let us think for future afterwards. At present let the business run as it is.'

I thought many things sitting in my room at nights. But I could not arrive at a decision. Lalaji was no more, so, I should not remain in shop, I thought. But no final decision came to my mind. What path will be for me now! I felt safe from all dangers remaining under the shadow of protection from Lalaji. He was truly my protector. One day his family will forget him. But I cannot forget him. Now I feel solitary and forlorn.'

At last I arrived at a decision – 'I shall leave this place after making Piku known all business tricks within a short period. Let Piku be a successful businessman. I shall keep Mataji's words. Mataji will decide about the partition of Lalaji's property between Ravi and Piku in time. I know, Mataji has wished me from her heart to make business with Piku together. I loved to work with Lalaji. But now situation is different without Lalaji.'

For two months I was busy to make Piku learnt all points properly in the business, in the same way I learnt from Lalaji. Munimji kept my salary in bank account as before. Expenditure for my monthly food in hotel was also paid. I taught Piku all the accounts of materials in godown with payable and getable details. I taught regarding companies to be dealt with taking all corresponding files. Piku was a commerce graduate, therefore, theoretical knowledge he had already. Now practical knowledge and experience was necessary. He would not get difficulty. Mataji had been signing in cheques. If she wanted Piku's name also could be included.

In my room I was listening to some news in transistor. Taking the diary I began to write – Death of Lalaji had given me a shock. He knew me well. His love and faith kept me to forget my past. I have decided to go to the Himalayas, but 'when' I will leave, not decided yet. Shravana's final examination in M.A. will be concluded in this month. I shall leave this place after her examination.

Now all members and relatives of Lalaji are slowly forgetting him. Everything now is going to be normal. But I feel his existence all the time. He was not only a business man but also he had many virtues and qualities. He knew my condition, hence he made me comfortable with his open discussions. He told me about personal matters of his family. Sometimes he talked with me so openly as if, I was his friend. One day he told me that there were some plans for future and he would bring them in reality with me. I will never know his plans now – death took away Lalaji.

I thought about Assam, 'How many people are dying every day there! One death gives how much sufferings to a family, only the sufferers can feel. How the Ministers, M.L.As and bureaucrats protected by security force can feel those heart – rending! How the governments which fail to give security to the general people, can feel humanitarian value! Leaders come in election time with crocodiles tears to beg for votes. Now a days people are going to lose faith in elections also. There is suspicion – whose votes will go to whose favour!'

Yesterday, the examination of Shravana was finished. Piku and I went to visit Sahashradhara. We came many times before, to visit here. Most probably today is my last visit to Sahashradhara to me. We went to Shravana's home on return from Sahashradhara. Seeing after few days, Aunty said,' All members of family are still grieved for the death of Lalaji. Normalcy will come slowly.'

'Everything is going well. I was none of Lalaji, but he was like my near and dear.' I said.

'Now let the citation of all sentimental matter be stopped. All the sorrows will be forgotten in the course of time.' Shravana said.

'Shravanaji let us leave all those things. Now, tell how you have done in exam. In fact, we have come to know about your exam.' I said.

'Well, I hope I will get first class.' She said.

'Very good, in the time of result, no one knows where we shall be. Therefore, some special items should be fed to us today itself.' I said.

Hearing my words they began to laugh. After a thought for some time, Shravana said, 'Kalkaji, have you listened songs of Hindi film Rudali? Voices are of Dr. Bhupen Hazarika, Lata Mangeskar and Asha Bhosle. Music is Dr. Hazarika's own.'

A bit loudly I said, 'Our Bhupen Hazarika! Actually after the death of Lalaji I have not listened songs. Dr. Hazarika's songs in Rudali are in same tune of our Assamese songs. Now don't delay, play the cassette of songs. Indeed, every song of Dr. Hazarika seems to come from his heart. His voice touches everyone's heart.'

Shravana played the cassette. Aunty entered kitchen to cook something for Piku and me. I was listening the songs keeping my eyes closed. In between, Shravana also went to kitchen for some time. During the play of the cassette Shravana asked me, 'Shall I bring eatables now or after the end of songs?'

'Songs are about to finish, bring slowly as you wish,' I said.

After the playing of songs, Aunty and Shravana brought eatable in plates for us. Seeing different eatables I said,' You have taken pain in making these. Tea and biscuits would do.'

"You have said to make a special one, for, you are not sure where you would stay after my examination result."

Smiles came to all. At the time of eating, I said.' All of you, Mataji, Piku made me felt living in a family when Lalaji was there. Now I feel empty without Lalaji.'

'Do not be sentimental again. Will you listen the songs again? You wanted to listen the song of the 'Aap ki kasam' film again one day,' Shravana said to me.

'We become very sentimental easily. Let the sentiment go now. Please play the cassette of the film.' I said to her.

Again all laughed. Shravana played the cassette smilingly. I listened the song *Karbate Badalte Rahe-- 'Aap ki Kasam'* being submerged. I was overwhelmed.

I said to her, 'Mind wants to go on listening the song. Today, we have listened a lot. Thank you for that.'

After this, Piku and I were ready to go. Piku started the motor bike. I was standing beside. I was seeing to the face of Shravana. I had seen a smile on her face. Lifting my right hand I said to her- 'Good bye.' I did not know why I had said so. She also reciprocated with words 'bye, bye' lifting her hand. I took my seat on bike. Piku drove away. We reached shop. I got down there and Piku drove home.

I had washed face and hands in my room. I had listened some news in the transistor. I opened a book but could not apply mind to read. I went out for a while. I came back to my room after taking meal in the hotel. Sitting on bed I thought – 'I am pleased to know that Shravana had expected well in her examination. Aunty and Mataji speak to me openly. Their behavior to me is like a member of the family. I do not know regarding the progress of marriages of Shravana or her elder brother. I have not asked anyone about this. I don't know why I had gazed at Shravana's face at the time of leaving her house. What has Shravana thought about me!'

Next day in the evening I went to Lalaji's house. First I bowed my head with folded hands to the picture of Lalaji, which was hung on wall. I talked to myself, 'Lalaji, forgive me. You have left all of us. So it is time for me to leave here and your home. I waited for restoration of normalcy in home for these months after your death.'

Mataji talked with me. Piku arrived after some time. Ravi had not come back yet. In between the talks, I said to Mataji, 'You should not be worried now. Piku can maintain everything properly hence forth.'

I did not give any indication of my final decision to them. I spoke to them with smiling face. Piku wanted to drop me in my room but I refused. I said,' I want to walk for some time. If I feel tired I shall go in an auto-rikshaw.' I departed from them. I got a glance of the car for the last time.

Entering my room first I kept my cloths in bag. Pass-book, cheque book, important documents, my diary and some books were taken in the bag. In bank I had amount of rupees in my account. I went to the hotel and took meal for the last time. I did not inform anyone about my decision of departure from here. Coming to room, I took pen and paper and began to write a letter to Mataji – Respected Mataji,

Accept my hearty respects. I spent two years as member of your family. I have decided to go towards the Himalayas, leaving you all. I thought to go after the death of Lalaji. But I waited for restoration of normal atmosphere in family. I wanted Piku to learn everything properly in two months. Now three months have passed from the time of death of Lalaji. Piku has equipped well. I could not dare speak to you about my decision to leave you. I have got pain in my heart for this. Lalaji knew everything about me. His death gave me a blow to my heart. I respected him earnestly. I shed tears for weeks silently. I felt myself solitary. I know, my departure will give you sorrow and grief. I will remember always your family along with Shravana's. I waited for the completion of Shravana's M.A. final examination. Do not know whether I can meet you in future. I am passing through an uncertainty. What will happen at last, it is in the hand of the fate. Of course, I have little faith in fate.

I had collected a great experience spending time in shop and business for these days. Lalaji had transacted lakhs of rupees through me in business. I have told Piku everything. I did not break confidence and faith, Lalaji kept upon me. I felt happy, when Lalaji said that he got benefit in business from some decisions taken upon my suggestions. Now I have faith on Piku and Ravi, that they will develop business further. Like some people, Lalaji also was not interested to invest money in stock market. He did not want to take risk in those investment. I don't know why, on my suggestions he bought shares of three companies for few thousands of rupees each. Now the markets of these companies are very good. It is hoped, that growth of money will be many times within four or five years. You are the nominee of the shares of the companies. I have told Piku what should be done for selling shares to lift money now after the death of Lalaji. You are not to be worried, Piku will maintain these.

You may think, why I have departed. I have an unknown attraction to the past stories and narratives of the Himalayas and presently about Badrinath, Kedarnath, Gongotri, Yamunotri, Kailash and Manash Sarovar (lake). From the days of the Ramayana and the Mahabharata, so many stories have been going on regarding the Himalayas. I have determined my mind to enter the inner side of unlimited natural beauty of the Himalayas. I also want to know about legends of great sages of the past. I left Assam due to some mental agony and social environment.

Lalaji had opened bank account for me, so that I did not spend money unnecessarily. So now with those money, I can maintain conveniently. From now on, please bar Munimji to deposit money in my bank account. This is my earnest request to you. I took meals with Lalaji and you in your home several times. It was like to me to take meal at my own home.

Again I cite that, I myself could not get courage to get farewell from you before my departure. Please forgive me.

Sincerely yours,
Kalkaji

I folded the letter and kept inside an envelope. I wrote on cover- To Mataji. It was midnight. I went to bed as I had to get up in morning. I did not get a good sleep at night. I had waked in early morning. I wore my cloth and also the jacket and kept a cap on head. There was not much cold. People would think, I was suffering from fever.

I told chowkidar Surendra previous night that I would go outside in the morning for some work. So, he did not doubt about me in the morning when I came out with my luggage. I told Surendra,' There is a letter to Mataji on my table in the room. Hand over the letter to Piku today and he will give it to Mataji.'

I kept fastening my bag on shoulder and another small bag by hand and in an autorikshaw I reached bus station. I kept covering my face with the cap so that others did not recognise me. I got into a Rishikesh bound bus and reached Rishikesh after half an hour.

Chapter-4

Swamji went on – After reaching Rishikesh it came to my mind, with Piku I came sometimes to visit temples and *ashram* at Rishikesh and Haridwar. So, they night come to find out me at Rishikesh. I thought it would be better for me not to stay in temples at Rishikesh. I decided to go to Debaprayag. Devaprayag is about seventy kilometers away from Rishkesh.

After few hours I reached Debaprayag by bus. I lodged in a pilgrim house of a temple. At afternoon I bought two pairs of saffron colored *dhotis* and *Kurtas* (long shirts) from market. Debaprayag is a nice small town. The river Alakananda and the Bhagirathi join here together and flow down unitedly taking the name Ganga.

There was many small beautiful places around Debaprayag. To visit Badrinath and Kedarnath, the road goes through Debaprayag. It is a religious place for the Hindus. It is said that king Dasharatha and Sriram had meditated here. There is a temple of Raghunathji in a rocky land, which is about some thousand years old. In 1803 year, Debaprayag town was damaged in earthquake. Bashistha Kunda (water hole) on the bank of the river Alakananda and Brahma Kunda on the bank of the river Bhagirathi were damaged. There is a faith amongst people that someone taking bath in the water at Baitashila place near Devaprayag, gets rid of the disease leprosy.

I started to wear saffron cloths at Devaprayag. I resided and took meal at the *ashram* of a temple. I familiarized with holy men and others in the temple. I began to take part in religious meetings. I got confidence on myself knowing their good impression upon me. I was attracted to a holy man there. More than half of his hair and beard were white. My regards grew towards him. With long hair and beard with saffron clothes, the holy man seemed to be the symbol of peace. His voice and movement were grave. Everyone called him Prabhuji. When I arrived here, Prabhuji named me Raghu. After few days intimacy grew between us. He called me lovingly Raghuji. I told Prabhuji about my desire to visit Badrinath and Kedarnath. He said, 'It is good to visit those pilgrimages. I have also not gone there for a few months. It will be better to accompany with you. You will not face difficulties. Along with other places, I am very familiar with four *dhams*. I have visited four *dhams* several times.'

I began to grow my hair and beard. Prabhuji said, ' Raghuji, you know English well along with Hindi. So you will be able to explain about spiritual wisdom of our religion to the foreign visitors.' Prabhuji sometimes called me as new holyman.

Prabhuji and myself spent about one and half month, visiting Badrinath and Kedarnath. It was very convenient to me with Prabhuji. First we visited Kedarnath. From Debaprayag we reached Srinagar. From Srinagar to Rudraprayag and then we reached Kedarnath. Our journey was through the bank of the Bhagirathi. I got some difficulties in walking from Shonganga and Gaurikunda to reach Kedarnath. We spent one week at Kedarnath. We visited all temples in Kedarnath *Dham*. We lodged in pilgrim house. Then we returned to Rudraprayag. We spent one week there staying in a pilrim house. From Rudraprayag we began our journey to Badrinath through the banks of the Alakananda. We stayed for ten days at Badrinath *dham*.

We visited all temples in Badrinath. River Basundhara falls in the Alakananda here. Prabhuji joined the religious gatherings in the temples. On his advice for one or two days I explained to the congregation of the devotees in English, translating from Hindi. At first stage I felt discomfort. Afterwards, I became accustomed to this. Prabhuji was well known to all, so no difficulty I found. Returning from Badrinath we reached Yoshimath. We stayed for one week at Yoshimath in a Pilgrim house of temple. Yoshimath is a beautiful place with natural scenery. Then we came to Nandaprayag. Here the Nandakini river falls in the Alakananda. Here also we stayed for one week. I learnt many things from Prabhuji for explaining the wisdom of Hindu religion to devotees. Many pilgrims from South India come to visit Badrinath and Kedarnth. I had to explain in English sometimes. Prabhuji was my guide and philosopher.

From Nandaprayag we came to Rudraprayag. Again we spent one week here. At Rudraprayag, river Mandakini falls in the Alakananda. It is a nice place. From here we came to Srinagar where we stayed for two days. And we reached Devaprayag after leaving Srinagar.

We stayed at Debaprayag in the *'ashram'* of a temple. Different matters were discussed with Prabhuji, about religion specially. After fifteen days I expressed my desire to Prabhuji to visit the Gongotri and the Yamunotri. Prabhuji said to me, 'We have just visited Badrinath and the Kedarnath. It is necessary to take rest for few days. You may suffer from illness, if you visit these cold places frequently. And now it is the month of November, the Gongotri and the Yamunotri will be closed for pilgrims after few days for six months due to coldness and snowfalls. We shall think to visit after few months. Now I have to go to Haridwar. You also come with me. We have visited the Badrinath and the Kedarnath before, it is good for us. All the four *dhams* remains covered with snow in winter season.'

I was puzzled in mind when Prabhuji told me to go to Haridwar with him. I could not say 'no' to him. I said, 'I like Rishikesh. I shall go to Rishikesh with you. You will go to Haridwar and I shall remain at Rishikesh. On your return from Haridwar, I shall accompany with you at Rishikesh.'

Following day evening we reached Rishikesh at 7pm. We lodged at a pilgrim house of a temple. Prabhuji was familiar with all temples and pilgrim houses at Rishikesh. He said, 'I shall remain one week at Haridwar. If you wish, you may come to Haridwar after two days.' He also informed me the address of the temple at Haridwar.'

Next day morning Prabhuji went to Haridwar. In the mean time, I was in fear of meeting someone from Dehradun. I suspected - Mataji, Piku or some other person could see me here. About three months had passed. I neither, cut my hair nor shaved beard on my own wish. I thought in this condition, no one could know me. Therefore, I found no difficulty to go outside. I had not told Prabhuji regarding my stay at Dehradun before or my departure from there.

I took bath in the Ganga along with Prabhuji in the morning. I wanted to see the area of the temple and pilgrim house. There was a hall in the temple for congregation of devotees. Ritual offerings of light were performed in the temple in the evening. Then moral principles of religion were explained to the devotees by one or more holymen.

On the walls of the hall, pictures of different gods and goddesses were hung. There was a big paper pasted on a wall. There were written – 'Kalkaji, hope you will return, if not, please speak on telephone at least.'

- Mataji and Shravana

Two telephone number also were written there. I knew these numbers were of Mataji and Shravan's house. They had written in this way! It made me nervous. I sat down on the floor. After a while I asked one devotee of the temple, 'How many days ago had that paper been pasted there?' I pointed out to the paper on wall. He replied, 'About three months have passed. Not finding Kalkaji, they had pasted the paper here. Do you know Kalkaji? 'I was silent. I only moved my head giving indication of 'no.'

I returned to my room in the pilgrim house. In the temple, they did not know me. They would have suspected me, had I removed the paper. Many questions arose to me – Had Mataji, Shravana and others aggrieved for leaving them? They were none of me, yet I was in hearty relationship with them. Should I now talk to Mataji and Shravana on telephone? After talking to them on telephone, should I go to Debaprayag? I thought- writing on paper and keeping it in temple was innovative work of Shravana. What type of situation comes to people!

Working with Lalaji for two years, it was a great experience to me. I had no prior experience, but I mastered every thing within one year from Lalaji. I could not leave Lalaji, had the death not come to him. Lalaji lamented – he could not make his two sons as per he wanted. One day I told Lalaji, 'In my mind, your two sons are good enough. They have no bad habit. They do not disobey you. Sons of many people become drunkards and drug addicted and run costly cars, spoiling hard earned money of parents. It is not true that having good academic results and good employment, one would be a good man.' Lalaji was in deep thought for a while hearing my words. Then he said to me, 'You have mentioned a very substantial remark. Your understandings are above your age.' I was happy hearing his remarks about me.

At last I had decided to talk to Mataji. She might not be at home during day time. She might be at shop. I thought, it would not be proper to talk to her at shop. So, I decided, it would be better to talk to her on telephone at home in the evening at 7 or 8 pm. But I was confused – what talk I would! They had, perhaps, forgotten me till now!

I came out to market in the evening. I did not want to talk to Mataji on telephone from the temple. Devotees in temple might think otherwise after knowing that myself was Kalkaji. I rang up Mataji from a telephone booth in the market.

-- Mataji, good evening ......

-- Who?

-- Myself...........

-- Kalkaji!

-- Yes, I am.

-- Where are you from speaking?

I did not want but still in mouth 'from Rishikesh' came out.

- In which place of Rishikesh you are?

- I am staying in a pilgrim house of temple.

- Where did you stay for so many days?

- In Debaprayag, then I visited Kedarnath and Badrinath.

- Tell me the name of the temple and room number if there is.

I could not resist myself not to mention the name of the temple and pilgrim house. I felt, it was my mother's command.

- Swear in my name, don't leave the place without informing us.

- I do ...., Mataji

Then I kept the telephone and returned to the temple after paying telephone talk charge. Religious discussion was going on at the temple. I was sitting there for some time.

I came to my room. It perplexed me at Mataji's words – 'do not leave the place without informing us.' What was the meaning of that? Was the meaning to call on them? Or, they would come here to see me! Mataji's words placed me in an awkward situation. I have lost courage to face them. It occurred to me – if I did not go to call on them within one or two days, they might arrive here. It would be better for me to leave Rishikesh without facing them. If they did not find me here, it would be a matter of distrust! Again I would be marked an escapist in their eyes. I pondered to take decision next day. I went to take meal in the dining hall of the pilgrim house. After taking meal, came to room and went to sleep on the bed at floor of the room.

Next day morning I was surprised to see Mataji, Aunti, Shravana and Piku. They arrived in the car at pilgrim house. They were sitting in the guest room. They felt discomfort seeing me with long hair and unshaved beard. Anxiety was written large on their faces. When I approached to touch the feet of Mataji and Aunty, Mataji said to me, 'You are now a holyman, do not touch our feet.' Yet I touched their feet with bowed head. I saluted Shravana with folded hands. Then I embraced Piku. I could not decide to begin where from. Shravana was also silent. She was deeply seeing to my face.

Mataji broke the silence. She said to me, 'Why did you left us giving pain and sorrow?'

I said, 'People cannot do things in spite of their expectation and some things happen without speculations. It does not matter consequences. In my case also, suppose, it happened in course of events.'

Then she asked me, 'When did you arrive at Rishikesh?'

I said, 'Day before yesterday evening I along with Prabhuji arrived here from Debaprayag. Prabhuji is the respected holyman in the monastery of the Temple at Debaprayag, where we have been staying. From Dehradun I reached Debaprayag. After staying for more than ten days there, I visited the Badrinath and the Kedarnath with Prabhuji. Yesterday morning, Prabhuji had gone to Haridwar.

Mataji said, 'We moved around Rishikesh and Haridwar to find you out. We did not get trace of you. Therefore, Shravana wrote on paper that way and pasted on walls of some temples. You have talked on telephone after you read now. Would you otherwise, talk?'

I said, 'I cannot forget all of you in my life. Eventually, I had talked to you. And today I have got an opportunity to meet you. I am grateful to Shravanji for this.'

Shravana asked me, 'What name have you taken now here?'

I said, "Prabhuji calls me Raghu. There is a very old temple in the name of Raghunathji at Debaprayag.

So, Prabhuji perhaps game me that name Raghu. But I shall remain as 'Kalkaji' to all of you.'

Shravana got up to go outside with Piku saying to Mataji and Aunty, 'You talk to Kalkaji. I am coming from outside with Piku.'

Mataji told me, 'We did not disclose some matters to you. Do you know who was most grief-stricken after you left?'

I was silent. I could not guess. Then Mataji said, 'It was Shravana.' My voice was loud, 'Shravana!'

Mataji again said, 'Yes, it was Shravana. You did not know – the boy whom Shravana had loved, married a girl of his own caste taking large amount of money in dowry. It is true, Shravana got aggrieved. But you said that the boy may not love her from his heart. And she got confidence on you. She got courage to continue her study. You were a good friend of hers. Your letter to me is kept by her. She was confident, that one day you would see the writings on papers in the temples. And now it has become true.'

Tears came out from the eyes of Mataji and Aunty. I remained speechless. In answer, what should I speak! Where to start!

After a long pause I said, 'Mataji, truly I had the thoughts of the Himalayas before. I had been in forgetful mood, staying with Lalaji.'

Mataji said, 'Lalaji had trusted you so much, that he consulted some matters with you first and we had come to know afterwards. Lalaji pretended, he wanted you to drink wine. We thought that Lalaji certainly would make you drink, but you did not. He could not. After the wine-incident, Lalaji had double faith on you. When Shravana and others knew about the acting story, they enjoyed humour saying – Lalaji could do everything, but he could not make Kalkaji drink wine. Have you done the good thing to leave us even after the death of Lalaji?'

I said, 'Mataji, it was difficult decision to leave all of you. You loved and believed me. So, my separation had made you aggrieved. But your affection and faith inspired me to get courage and to think you as my nears and dears.'

Shravana and Piku returned. Some Papers were in Sharavan's hand. Showing the papers she said to me, 'Kalkaji, these papers were to find any information regarding you. I kept these papers in some temples. I have taken some of them. Again these will be necessary if you become traceless. Devotees of the temples have known now, when I took away the papers.'

I said, 'I am overwhelmed with the way to trace out a missing person. For this novel skill, credit must go to Shravanaji.' On my remarks, they smiled faintly.

Shravana said to me, 'Now you will meet sages and holymen in the Himalayas. Therefore, sharpness of tongue and expression will increase certainly. Hope, one day you will be a preceptor.'

I felt a concurrence of anger and resentment in her voice. Defending myself I said to her, 'Preceptor! You have said about a preceptor. Firstly, I have doubt on myself to become a good disciple.'

Mataji understood, the debate between me and Shravana should not proceed further. She changed the topic. She said to me, 'Perhaps, you do not know that Lalaji had built the second storey for you and Piku. He wanted you to be a partner of our business. I also wanted, but suddenly you had left us secretly.'

I said, 'Mataji, I have neither attraction nor greed to property and money. Make proper exploit of Lalaji's property and money. Let the business flourish further. This is my utmost wish. I pray to The God always for sound health and hale to all of you.'

Mataji asked, 'Is it your final decision to spend the life of a holy man? What is the obstacle in returning from this path? The path you have chosen, is hard and troublesome. Still there is time now, try to contemplate once deeply.'

I replied, 'Mataji, suppose, you have three sons. Your two sons are running business. Your other son wants to go outside to find out the truth of life in this earth. He wants to discover some mysteries of the Himalayas. Please do not prevent me. Though I don't remain near you, my bondage of relationship of heart, will remain intact.'

I had seen their eyes were moist. It seemed that they would cry now. Somehow, I obstructed my tears. Stillness was around.

Then my voice sounded, 'Shravanaji.' I stopped. 'What should I speak to her?' Shravana reciprocated, 'Yes, please speak.'

Controlling my emotion, I said, 'Today I feel very happy to meet you all. For this, I am grateful to all of you.'

Again there was silence. Shravana said, 'Kalkaji, I have a request to you for me.'

I gazed at her face. She continued, 'Don't be frightened. We don't compel you to come back against your wish.'

I felt relieved. I said, 'Please, order me, I must obey.'

She said, 'You left Dehradun in secret, giving us pain and sorrow. Swear in my name, please keep informing us where ever you stay now onwards. Also inform, where and when you would go from here.'

I said, 'You have applied another responsibility upon me. You have kept me bound by obligation now. I give you word, I shall keep you communicating.'

I observed naturalness on Shravana now.

She said, 'It is not possible to exchange letters in the Himalayas. But wherever telephone- facilities are there, please communicate. Or would there be an excuse of forgetting our telephone numbers?'

'No, no, it will not happen.' I said.

I remembered M.A. examination of Shravana.

I asked her, 'Shravanaji, I have not asked you an important subject...... Had the result of examination been out?'

She did not reply to me. She was silent and remained absent minded.

Aunty said, 'Last week her result had come out. She has got first class. Result is nice, but she has no enthusiasm.'

I repeated to myself – 'Result is nice, but she has no enthusiasm.'

I got a sense of doubt. To make the situation easier, I said, 'Shravanaji, I am very delighted to know your exam result. Now you can get a service or, you do Ph.D.'

Shravana did not respond to me. She looked towards Mataji and Aunty. Mataji comprehended discomfort on Shravana.

Mataji said, 'Kalkaji, let us depart now. We have expressed our views. Try to think over again.'

I said, 'Nobody knows what is stored on his fate. Please do not take my journey as never to return.'

It was time to bid them farewell. It was painful to me.

I said, 'Please wait for a while. Let me bring '*prasad*' (light food offered to deity) from the temple'

I went to temple to bring 'p*rasad*'. I came back with *prasad* and offered to them. No one uttered a word. I had seen on their faces ignorant looks to me. They had taken 'Prasad' but unwillingly and absent – mindedly.

After a while, they proceeded to the car to get in. They took their seats. Shravana kept a profound look at me. Piku switched on car and the car started to run. I lifted my right hand to bid good-bye to them. I was seeing to the car till it was beyond my sight.

I came to my room and sat down. Many thoughts came to mind – 'What impression on me they had taken!' I questioned myself- 'Would it have better not to ring Mataji?' Had I not talked to Mataji on telephone, I would not have been to face this situation today!

I should have kept myself distant from them without information. New state of discomfort and pain would not have come to them today again. Which one is right! Which one is wrong! I felt myself too weak to judge those.

I had come to know from the day's happening- 'Mataji and others still have love and fondness of me as before.' I rciterated to myself,' Lalaji wanted me to be a partner of his business, wanted me to live in the second story, Sharvana's loved youth married another girl for the greed of dowry. I was her good friend, her good result in M.A. examination'- all these things I had come to know from them today. Why did Mataji say- 'Shravana was the most aggrieved in my departure.' Perhaps, I had broken the faith of friendship. Possibly, Shravana could not tolerate easily my secret disappearance.

Four days passed from the day Mataji and others' coming to Rishikesh. I went out to the bank of the Ganga in morning and evening. I spent time sitting there. I also spent time in temple. Prabhuji would come in a day or two. I felt grieved. Sitting on the bank at evening, I observed running water flow of the Ganga. The Ganga was flowing silently. Recollection of my past came to me...... I left my home after the death of Apu and Aruba. I felt a fresh hurt in me. I was also partially guilty for their deaths. Apu could not become a doctor, Aruba passed M.Sc. with fame, but deaths came to them. Suddenly an utterance came to my mouth – "Shravana!' I was frightened... Aruba suffered from depression and absent-mindedness after the death of Apu and the incident of APSC oral examination. And then death came to her. It struck my mind ..... 'Shravana also might suffer from....' 'That day did I observe such symptoms in her? I asked myself. If something unknown happened to her like that of Aruba! Anxiety transformed to panic in me. I proceeded fast to speak to Shravana from the telephone in the temple.

I rang up Shravana's house on telephone number. She lifted telephone.

_Sharavanaji, good evening..........

_Good evening.

_I am Kalkaji speaking....

__I know. But Kalkaji or Raghuji speaking? And where from?

_Suppose both of them. I am speaking from the temple in Rishikesh. Are you and others okay at your home?

__All are OK. But why you have asked? How do you remember me?

__That day after you left, an anxiety was in my mind. You were absent - minded.

_Anxiety! For yourself or for others?

_No anxiety to myself, but for you....

_Where are you going from Rishikesh? For how many days you will stay there?

__Prabhuji may return from Haridwar in one or two days. I did not go to Haridwar. I shall return to Debaprayag with him.

___Do not forget to speak to me before your departure.

_Certainly, I will not forget.

I kept the telephone. I was now a relieved person. Anxiety and panic in my mind vanished. Shravana was well. Again one thought came to mind- 'If something happens to her! Anxiety resurfaced to me. I never tried to know her mind. I always kept a distance from her. She also kept the distance. Now I have come to know – some happenings take course on their own. Shravana is a grave girl. It is difficult to understand a grave girl. For this, talent is also necessary. Why these thoughts have come to mind now! I consoled myself – these are temporary sentiments, everything will be normal slowly. I have to keep my determination in mind.'

After two days Prabhuji returned from Haridwar. I felt embarrassed before Prabhuji. I was in very discomfortable position for the happenings of the past few days. Prabhuji read my state of mind from his experience. He asked me, 'Raghuji, are you worried? Have you faced some problem?'.. At last I said to Prabhuji everything openly. How I left Assam and spent two years at Dehradun with Lalaji, what type of relationship with Lalaji's family – I narrated all these. I also said about Shravana. And I told him about the arrival of Mataji, Aunty, Shravana and Piku at Rishikesh to meet me and about the talks with them in details. How Shravana kept papers with writings in temple- walls and my telephonic talk with Mataji – I narrated to him.

Prabhuji was hearing me silently. He did not ask me any question. He was busy in deep thought. I said to him, 'Shravana wanted a talk with me in telephone before we leave Rishikesh.' Prabhuji said after a thought, 'Everything will be all right. It will be better for us to stay for another two or three days here. Let us move around Rishikesh. You can speak to Shravana afterwards.' Then both of us went to temple.

In evening we were sitting on the bank of the Ganga. He said to me, 'My mind feels free now after knowing all about you. I hoped, you would tell me everything. From today a heavy burden is removed from your head. But the burden is not removed completely. Other heavy burden also may come on your way. So, do not lose your heart.'

After some time we came back to temple and joined the religious congregation.

After taking meal at pilgrim house we put to sleep. But I could not sleep. I gazed upon the day's conversations with Prabhuji. He had not tell me anything about his own till now. Perhaps, one day he would tell. His arrival had removed my anxiety and apprehensions. I thought, 'To become a holyman, great patience and courage are necessary. Difficulties are to be faced......' In the past, many of sages empowered themselves with great knowledge and immense energy in the strength of meditation. They had knowledge and wisdom of the past and the future. They had accumulated unlimited wisdom and energy. I thought, 'To become an ordinary monk or devotee will be enough for me?

Following day, it was more surprising for me. Piku and Sharavana arrived at pilgrim house. I was very embarrassed to see them. Anything ominous!

Shravana said, 'You are surprised to see me here again. Suppose, it is a surprise- visit.'

--- 'Surprise visit! But......' I uttered.

--- Buts are there certainly.

--- I was to speak to you before my departure.

--- You have not departed from here. I have come in confidence.

--- Do Mataji and Aunty know your coming here?

--- I am not a small girl now. I can take decision on my own.

--- What decision?

--- Are you frightened to hear the decision? Seeing no hope of your return to Dehradun, I myself have decided to go to your place.

--- What do you mean?

--- Yes, it is the Himalayas.

--- 'To the Himalayas...... you!' I shouted

--- 'Don't be afraid of. Today itself I shall not go. I have some works. I shall arrive here after two weeks. Then take me with you from here.' she said.

I said to her, 'You have parents and others in your family. How will Mataji and parents tolerate your separation? Think over again, please. Can you guess the consequences of your such a big decision?'

She said,' I have desisted all obstructions courageously and have succeeded. Now, don't obstruct me, please. You have also chosen the path without pondering over consequences.'

I could not reply. I was quiet for a while.

Suddenly, I was alert at Prabhuji's voice. I did not notice that he was nearby. He said, 'It is hoped by all, that consequences will be good. No one expects those to be evil.'

I introduced Prabhuji to Sharavana and Piku. Both of them bowed with folded hands to Prabhuji. Shravana said,' Prabhuji, that day Kalkaji, I mean, Raghuji told us about you.'

Prabhuji said,'He has been staying with me for last three months. I have named him Raghu. But lovingly call him Raghuji. Yesterday, I have come to know about you and others from him. I am of the age of your father. Shravana, think over again about your decision. How much unsafe and trouble- some might be the path for you!'

Sharvana said, 'Prabhuji, do not block my path, please. As I am a woman, you have doubt in my courage and patience. Are not there many woman devotees or holy women in the Himalayas?'

After a thought Prabhuji said to Sharvana,' Knowing you and your firmness, some recollections of my past have come to me.'

Then Prabhuji narrated – There was my dear daughter named Swati. She wanted not to be married off. She wanted to do government service. Her mother died when she was reading in high school. She was an intelligent student. Before taking degree from college I told her- 'I shall not always remain with you. I can die happily if you are married off to a boy of a good family.' After she took graduation degree, in spite of her unwillingness, I gave her in marriage to a good service-holder boy on my insistence. I was in service. She was my only child. I spent much money in her marriage. I presented many household items to my daughter in her marriage. First year ran well. But the parents-in-law of my daughter demanded more money from me. To the family, which I thought to be good one, married off my daughter. But the family could be so greedy, I could not imagine. They again demanded that my land and house be transferred in their son's name. They suspected, I might hand over my property in the name of somebody else. Informed them that I would not transfer my property to anybody before my death. After my death, all my property would go to Swati. They started harassment and ill-treatment on Swati on the ground that, why I had not transferred my property to their son. I felt ashamed to introduce their son as my son-in-law. He was like a spineless servant of his parents. I repented for giving Swati in marriage to such a boy of an evil family. I came to know about the ill-treatments inflicted on her by the family, from her letters. What she wanted! What she had now got! They did not allow her to come to my home. She sent letters secretly to me. I decided – once she would have arrived at my house, I would never allow her to return.

But I could not take her to my home. Before that, one day I got the evil news – 'Swati was badly burnt.' She fought against death in hospital. She gave statements to police that her parents-in-law set fire on her. Seeing her sad face and tragic condition I could not stop my uninterrupted flow of tears. Her voice became feeble. I understood what she wanted to speak-'father why did you get me married off?'

After three days Swati died. I lodged FIR in police station. For how many days I should run to the court with lawyers! Our judiciary is slow and motionless. How much pain we are to bear to make the guilty punished! Had the police investigated cases impartially, many would have got justice. Gradually, Swati's case was forgotten. I knew, my daughter's soul would not rest in peace, if the guilty were not punished. Sometimes I thought of taking revenge. I wanted to do so something but I might become unsuccessful. I might be caught and then I would be jailed! But then it came to my mind, Swati's soul would be sad doubly.

The employed boys who do not want to give maintenance expenses to their married wives but become greedy for the properties of the parents of wives, are stains in our society. The boys along with their families are more guilty. After the marriage, duty and responsibility of a man fall on him for his wife. But there are also many self respected boys and families, who do not greed for others' property. Prabhuji again said, 'Memories of Swati gave me pain and sorrow all the time. I took voluntary retirement from service. I sold my land and house and kept the money in bank. One day I came out to the Himalayas and moved directionlessly. I visited four *'dhams'*- the Badrinath, Kedarnath, Gongotri and Yamunotri. Thereby, I had taken the form of a holyman. I had spent several years in this path. I donated small money to the temples. There are very cheap food and lodging in pilgrim houses. Now a days the places are known to me. In some pilgrim houses food and lodging are free.

'I spent most of the years at Debaprayag. I do not know, why I bought two *kathas* of land on the bank of the Alakananda from a person. I thought, after moving and visiting temples, I shall, one day, take rest in my own cottage on the land. But till now, no cottage has been built there. Again thought came to me, what I shall do building the cottage! I shall donate the land to temple. Suddenly, unknowingly, one day Raguhuji arrived there from somewhere. Now I have thought to build the cottage there after meeting Raghuji. I did not ask anything to him. If I ask, he may be worried- I thought. Now I have come to know everything about him. It will be a help to me, if he does not go away to other places. I do not know, what in Raghuji's mind.'

Prabhuji was tired after speaking all these time. Tears came out into his sad face. Getting up from her seat Shravana wiped the tears from Prabhuji's face with the end of her cloth. I remained speechless hearing his past story and seeing tears on his eyes.

Prabhuji said to Shravana, 'I did not allow Swati to continue her studies and got her married off against her wish. I have been suffering till now for my wrong doing. You are highly educated girl, you have succeeded to be determined in your path. It is natural for your Kalkaji to become very anxious for your step in this difficult path. But the result of blocking one's determination by force, might be costly and opposite. But, Sharvana, will you be able to overcome the hindrance from your parents?'

Shravana replied, 'In this matter, I argued with them strongly. They insisted me on my marriage. I told them firmly that, I would never get married. If Kalkaji can be a holyman, why not me a holy woman? I have great faith on Kalkaji – hence I dare step in this thorny track. Prabhuji, you are there now, so no question of dread and doubt would arise surely. You are now our godfather. Assume, your lost Swati has returned in me.'

Prabhuji applauded, 'It is a great day today for me. Three months back, your Kalkaji came out as if my son to me in Debaprayag and today you have appeared before me as if my daughter in Rishikesh.

Truly by the grace of god, for my some virtuous act, I have found both of you.'

A bright smile appeared on Prabhuji's face. He happily said, 'Let us now take midday's meal together at the pilgrim house.'

We proceeded to the dining hall of the pilgrim house. We did not talk much during taking meal. Then we returned to the guest room.

Prabhuji began to speak, 'Shravana, as you have moved forward this much, I do not hinder you. Your parents would get pain for few days, after your abandonment of home. Gradually naturalness would appear in your home. It is natural to get pain and sorrow in separation. You have wanted to come, after two weeks finishing your personal works. Keep with you important things and some books. In future, both of you have to study religious books and to preach wisdom. You are to practice and learn scriptures and thereby to make a habit of learning.'

We were listening to Prabhuji with great attention. To ask a question I said to him, 'Prabhuji, I think…….'

Before I could complete my question, Prabhuji said to me, 'Now don't be disheartened. I am like father to both of you, but your learning and education are better than me. You are a pious devotee and Shravana is on her way. For each other, you will remain a grand seat of inspiration. You are to master patience, self-retrain and courage. You are to remain alert in every step, for present holy places are not like the those of the yore. There are crooked lookings of the evil minded. Many tourists had polluted and disgraced the sanctity of holy places and pilgrimage. I shall remain as a help to you for the days I live. And I hope to visit four 'dhams' with you again.'

Piku was silently hearing our conversations till now. He said to me,

'Kalkaji, Mataji has asked me to deposit some money in your bank account. She also has told me to inform you not to fight shy to tell us whenever you need money.'

I said, 'The money presently I have, will take many days to be spent. How much money would be necessary for austere living! Do not deposit money in my bank account. I have no desire for money.'

He said, 'Mataji's fear is that, if you do not transact your account for one or two years your account number will be closed by the bank. You will face difficulty if you cannot withdraw money when you need. There is need for treatment of illness No one can say what would happen tomorrow. Uncle had opened a bank account in sister Shravana's name yesterday.'

I said, 'I have found no word to thank Mataji and you. As a token of love for you, I offer a condition that, you will deposit one hundred rupees half yearly in my account. And my bank account will not be closed then. It will not be easy for uncle and

Aunty to endure sorrow in Shravana's part with. Opening an account in her name, they want a little peace in their minds.'

Piku said, 'I shall inform Mataji about all matters. I can't say whether Mataji accept your condition or not.'

It was silence for a while. Breaking the silence Prabhuji said to me, 'Mataji and others accepted you as their near related one. So, they are aggrieved at your separation. In the same way, it is natural to get hurt to Shravana's parents at her separation. Disunion comes after union and union comes after disunion. This is one of our human natures. It is intolerable agony to the parents to be separated from their children. Your parents also got that agony.'

It was time for departure to Shravana and Piku. Prabhuji said, 'If Sharvana remains adamant to her decision, then select an auspicious day. Raghuji will communicate to Shravana in these days. For, there may be problems for her. It is another matter, if Shravana changes her decision in between.'

At the departing time Shravana said to me,' Don't think, I am going to change my decision. I shall arive here after two weeks positively.'

Prabhuji had gone towards the temple. I went to the car with them. Piku started the car. Shravana sat in the car keeping a deep sight on my face. The car moved away.

I said to myself – 'I don't know how many unknown realties are with Shravana!'

I remained sitting on the bank of the Ganga for some time. After coming to room, I saw Prabhuji already was there. After a short while he said to me, 'You may think why I have not discourage Shravana. I noticed, she was firm in her decision. Her parents urged her for marriage. She refused with courage. It was you from whom she got inspiration of courage. In this case if you or I prevent her, there may happen an unexpected incident. Then will you be able to bear with? She has wanted to remain a companion with you. If she comes, she is to be a devotee in the temple of the 'ashram' at Debaprayag and to remain in woman pilgrim house. Accepting this path, you are to visit four 'dhams'and other religious places.'

After three days, we departed to Debaprayag, I talked to Shravana on telephone on the evening of the previous day before our departure. Shravana herself had fixed the day. There was not much talk between Prabhuji and me in the journey. Being seated many thoughts came to my mind, when our bus was passing through the bank of the Ganga. I thought, 'Shravana at the end, will change her decision. I would have been happy enough if she had changed her decision. I did not give any indication to Prabhuji regarding my thoughts. I expected Prabuji's presence would relieve me of my worries.'

The day before the fixed day I came to Rishikesh from Debaprayag. I was in anxiety in these days at Devaprayag. I have to proceed with Shravana through an uncertainty. Prabhuji said to me, 'Go alone and bring Shravana to Debaprayag from Rishikesh. You can talk openly to her.'

I arrived at the pilgrim house of the temple, where I previously lodged. The night was wakeful for me. I thought, 'I should have prevented Shravana from coming to this path.' Again it came to mind, 'If some unexpected event happens to her as Probhuji suspected!' Memories of Apu and Aruba were brought back to me.

Following morning this time also Piku brought her in car. I knew, 'How Mataji or her parents can come with her! No parent want their sons or daughters to become ascetics. Shravana's parents were subdued by her hard decision! But their grief can't disappear so early from their hearts, the grief of separation of Shravana from them.'

We spoke for a while in the guest - room of pilgrim – house. Speaking Piku and me to go out of the room Shravana said, 'Let me change the cloths.' After few minutes she came out with saffron dress (*salower* and *kamij*) and covered her head with the light coloured shawl. I gazed at her for few moments in that new appearance. A sign of anxiety also appeared on the face of Piku. Shravama said,

'I made two pairs of saffron dresses without the knowledge of my parents. How much they would have aggrieved, had they seen me in the saffron dress! So I have changed my clothes here. They at least have not seen me in the new form of saffron dress.'

Piku took us in the car to the bus station. He unloaded two bags of Shravana from the car. We were waiting near Piku. A picture of grief appeared to his face. Embracing him I said, 'Let us meet again. Do not be sorry. Keep going on your business well.'

Shravana said to him affectionately, 'Drive carefully.'

We got in the Debaprayag bound bus. Piku loaded the bags in bus. Our bus started to run. We bade him farewell. He reciprocated lifting his hands. We kept him seeing until he was out of sight.

Shravana was viewing the natural scenes outside through the window of bus single - mindedly. She was sitting in the left seat to me. It had struct to my mind still – 'how did Shravana choose this journey with so much courage!' We were near but still very far! Our bus had stopped occasionally. She was seeing to my face. Then she said, 'Kalkaji, in the past or even now also, it is said, that the Kedarnath, Badrinath, Gongotri and Yamunotri are on the way to the heaven. These four *'dhams'* are called to be near the heaven. In those days it was very difficult to visit four *'dhams'* or the Kailash. That is why, perhaps, four *'dhams'* were called gateways to the heaven. The heaven is, perhaps, imaginary! But the Himalayas, four *'dhams'*, the Kailash and Manas Sarovar – these are true. The Ganga, the Yamuna, the Alakananda and the Mandakini – these rivers are also true.'

I was hearing to her attentively. I tried to reply. But before that, Shravana spoke, 'King Bhagirath brought the goddess Ganga down from the heaven to the earth with the sound of conch.'

I said gravely, 'And today Kalkaji is taking Shravanaji by bus from Rishikesh to Devaprayag.'

I found a glitter of smile on Shravana's face. After a thought, she said, 'Kalkaji, I wish to touch you once.'

I gazed at her, she seized my hand by her hands and began to gaze at my face unwinkingly. I was very embarrassed. I was staring at her pair of eyes. I saw on her luminous face,- a supreme angle of vision and a divine power. On her whole face I perceived a sight of amazing beauty of a goddess. I wanted to touch the goddess who possessed wonderful lustre. I kept my right hand on the forehead of the goddess. Utterance came to my mouth, 'Goddess Shravana!' Hearing my voice the goddess seemed to wake up. Shravana returned to reality. She said to me,' I don't know where from I got the courage to walk into this endless path. But there must be an apprehension of uncertain fear. What do you think?'

I said, 'What ever fear and uncertainty are there, Prabhuji with remove.

He is now our *guru*, the spiritual guide.'

'Why did Prabhuji not come with you to Rishikesh?' She asked me.

'The *guru* sends his disciple first to perform rituals to drive away evils. If the disciple becomes unsuccessful, then the *guru* takes his own steps.' I said.

'Then I can contemplate – the disciple has become successful in the battle of religious crisis.' She said.

'Not only the disciple but also the lady disciple with me, is equal partner for the success in the war for peace.' I said,

'Kalkaji, did you study literature before? Being a student of science also, you can speak easily adding ornamental words of language – literature.' She said after thinking for some time.

'I am practicing a little. It will be necessary in future to study religion and scriptures. At the same time I might have to debate with the goddess Shravana.' I said.

A smile appeared on Shravana's face. She said. 'I have said before, king Bhagirath brought the goddess Ganga to the earth from the heaven. Now I like to say – god Kalka is leading the goddess Shravana towards the heaven. Of course, I am not a goddess.'

Smile appeared to me at her words slightly. Shravana said in a rising voice, 'I have seen a smile in the grave face.'

I said, 'Perhaps, this is the smile of happiness – for the auspicious moments at the arrival of the goddess Shravana at Debaprayag from Rishikesh.'

We had arrived at Debaprayag. Talks between us had come to an end. We proceeded to the temple. Prabhuji was in the temple. We bowed to him with folded hands. I kept Shravana's two bags near.

Prabhuji uttered, 'At last Shravana has arrived at the path to the Himalayas.'

He introduced her to other devotees. And then he said to me, 'Tell yourself what the better name should be bestowed to the new devotee.'

I said, 'Shravana-Devi, that is, goddess Shravana.' Hearing the new name all were pleased.

Prabhuji expressed enthusiastically, 'Excellent title – Shravana Devi.' Shravana's staying was decided to be in the pilgrim house with another lady devotee in a room.

……..Two moths passed. Gradually Shravana was accustomed to the arduous life. Prabhuji said, 'I think, God had sent Raghuji before and now Shravana to me. You are my God sent children.'

Gradually we could talk about all matters openly. Our hesitation was removed till now. I thought, 'Shravana does not know my past, so she might keep suspicion about me.' I myself said everything to her about me one day.

She said,' You may get hurt, so I did not ask about you. Now I am very happy for, I had come to know your past.'

I said, 'Our suspicion is removed. So, I have no objection if you read my diary too.'

She said, 'I shall read your diary afterwards. Transparency between us from now, will inspire us to study learning and philosophy. Had you written something objectionable about me?'

I replied with a smile,' You will come to know after reading.'

One day Prabhuji took us to the bank of the Alakananda to show his land. Prabhuji said, 'I told you before. I wanted to donate the piece of my land to some temple. Now I have thought, that the piece of land was waiting for you for those years. I have seen disputes for property in several temples and pilgrim-houses.

There is also honesty in many temples. But do not think, that, all of them are honest.'

I asked him, 'Prabhuji, why did you buy the land on the bank of the Alakananda instead of the Bhagirathi or the Ganga?'

Prabhuji said, 'I did not select the land for choice. Of course, you cannot take land anywhere according to your choice. The Alakananda is flowing from the Badrinath *dham*. The Mandakini coming from the Kedarnath *dham* falls in the Alakananda at Rudraprayag. Here the Bhagirathi coming from the Gongotri falls in the Alakananda and they flow together to the plain, taking the name the Ganga. I have seen the natural scenes very fascinating from the land on the banks of the Alakananda. Now I have a thought to build a cottage. In future, you will build a bigger one. Do not worry about money. I had transferred my Bank account from Kanpur when I was at Haridwar. My Bank account is still at Haridwar.'

We returned to the pilgrim house after a short while.

At the end of April, Prabhuji said to me, 'Now, four *'dhams'* will be opened for pilgrimage. You also wished to visit the Gongotri and the Yamunotri dhams. Shravana has also not visited any place. Let us visit first the Gongotri and the Ymunotri After that, we shall visit again the Badrinath and the Kedarnath with Shravana,'

……….We spent the whole month of May visiting the Gongotri and the Yamunotry through the banks of the Bhagirathi and the Yamuna respectively. Both *dhams* are collection of flawless natural beauty. I had also seen the nature's amazing contribution to the Badrinath and the Kedarnath. Shravana was overwhelmed seeing the beautiful sources of the Ganga and the Yaumua. All of us were bewildered seeing the snow-clad illusionary peaks. Prabhuji had come before, for two or three times to the Gongotri and the Yamunotry. On the face, there was a peaceful and grave expression. I had imagined – God had created the mysterious Nature of the Himalayas.

Shravana said,' I have deserted the family members and to visit myself around the Himalayas with you. I had pained myself, leaving them grief-stricken. I had association with you and now Prabhuji too, as if a new family. Now the miraculous majesty of the Gongotri and the Yamunotri have made me forget my preceding sorrows.'

I remarked, 'That is why, there is written in scriptures – vision of the Himalayas makes people enduring and wise. It brings courage to mind.'

Hearing my words, Prabhuji said,' This is the primary lesson for the Himalayan spectacle. If you know how to search well, you collect various valuable matters in the Himalayas.'

We went to the Gongotri first from Debaprayag through Tehri and Uttarkashi. Returning from the Gongotri, we arrived at Dharabu and through Barkot we reached the Yamunotri. Our journey to both the pilgrimages were full of unprecedented and unique beauty. We had to walk few kilometers in both places. We walked but we did not feel tired. At the presence of Prabhuji, we travelled unperturbedly. We stayed in the pilgrim houses without any inconvenience. Prabhuji told us at the beginning,' In places of pilgrimage in the Himalayas, there might be evil minded people in the guise of holymen. So, be careful.'

We returned to Debaprayag. Shravana had talked to her home only twice in these months. I said to her, 'Sometimes talk to your family members. Then, they will feel comfortable in their minds hearing your voice,' One day she, informed Mataji and to her mother regarding the pilgrimage to the Gongotri and the Yamunotri.

Prabhuji and myself had prepared to build a small cottage. Keeping the front side vacant, the cottage was built on back side. The cottage was made of wood and corrugated iron sheets. Prabhuji was delighted. The cottage was made on Probhuji's desire. Most of the time Prabhuji and myself were busy with the workers. Shravana often came to see the work. The boundary of the land was fenced with ordinary wooden plank. I supervised the works at morning and afternoon. Rest of the time I spent in the temple. In about three months the work of the Cottage was completed.

Prabhuji said, 'The cottage has been built, but we can't stay here. My desire was to make the simple cottage. To stay in the cottage, some related works are to be done. Let it be there as a token. I feel happy with the thought of doing something at the piece of my land.'

I had a doubt – what others would think about! What for it is a necessity of land and house for a holyman! Prabhuji himself had removed my doubt. He said,' The temple and pilgrim-house where we live at present had grown to this stage from an ordinary piece of land and simple hut. Does a holyman or devotee not need of his own shelter? Now a days, most of the temples and pilgrim-houses have been used as places of business. A large part of donations and contributions is spent by functionaries for their own interest. How many trusts of temples and pilgrim houses are working selflessly in India? In the name of holy men, they are actually big traders collecting money and properties. They spend luxurious and sinful lives cheating people. Now I think about for your responsibility than mine. Does the responsibility of children not exist upon the father? Sometimes we shall take leisure in the cottage.'

I was deeply influenced by Prabhuji's words – Prabhuji is a widely experienced holyman of eminence, wisdom and consciousness. I thought, 'Shravana and myself have to step carefully, so that our words do not hurt Prabhuji. He has kept simple faith on us. We are to remain conscious always. His faith upon us must not be broken ever. It seems that Prabhuji has found a new home. Shravana and I are the new members of Prabhuji's home and family. From now onwards, it is our responsibility for Prabhuji. He has taken us as his near and dear. We must not commit faults in showing respects and regards to Prabhaji.'

.........At the end of the month of September we departed to visit Badrinath and Kedarnath. Prabhuji had visited several times before. I also visited few month back with Prabhuji., This time primary reason was for Shravana's visit. I said to Prabhuji after visiting the Gongotri and Ymunotri, about wish to visit to Badrinath and Kedarnath. Prabhuji said, 'We spent one month in visiting the Gongotri and

Yamunotri. You are new in the hilly and mountainous environment of the Himalayas. I am accustomed. So, take rest for, one or two months. I thought, before our visit to the Badrinath and Kedarnath the works for the cottage would be completed. But it took three months.'

This time we first visited Badrinath. Shravana said, 'I thought, before, that aged people should visit four *'dhams'* for pilgrimage. But now I think, no limit of age is required for pilgrimage.'

We went through the banks of the Alakananda to Badrinath by bus. Shravana observed minutely the temples and other things in Badrinath. The scenery of the mountains around had made illusive beauty. The Hemganga river falls in the Alakananda at Gobindaghat. Natural view of the Alakanda and the Nandakini mesmerizes people. We stayed at Badrinath for one week. To go to the Kedarnath we arrived at Rudraprayag. After staying for two days at Rudraprayag, we started our journey through the bank of the Mandakani to visit the Kedarnath by bus. After visiting the Kedar temple, we enjoyed the beauty of mountains and peaks from Kedarnath. Staying with Prabhuji, we did not find any inconvenience. On the advice of Prabhuji, we did not stay at small holy places in return journey. We also did not visit other places on the way to Kedarnath except at Rudraprayag. Prabhuji said to me. 'Last time you and myself were, so we could stay any where. This time Shravana is with us. So we should not waste time staying at small places.' Shravana wrote in her diary about the two *'dhams'* during our staying days there. She also wrote before, in details about the Gongotri and the Yamunotri pilgrimages. After about three weeks we returned to Debaprayag.

Four *'dhams'* were pleasing to eyes and heart touching for us.

After returning from the Kedarnath and the Badrinath our work load had increased. Prabhuji started primary lesson to study religion and scriptures for Shravana and me. We were also busy in work of the temple and the monastery. Our cottage was seemed to be turned into a school house. For, at day time Prabhuji, Shravana and I began to study different important matters at the cottage.

Prabhuji said, 'I have said before, if you know to search well, many valuable things you would find here in the Himalayas. On the whole way to the Badrinath and the Kedarnath, you will find various trees – small to big ones. In the same way you will find on the ways to the Gongotri and the Yamunotri – with the source of the most sacrosanct water. In the water and the land of the rivers and the rivulets, you will find many beneficial matters. You will find on granary of beneficial herbal medicines in the trees and shrubs. It is difficult in searching of them. These are cited in the old scriptures also. There are such hermits in some places in the Himalayas, who have the knowledge of these plants. I had also met one or two such hermits.'

I mentioned the cottage as a school house, for schools remained open in days and closed at nights. Different subjects were discussed for at least three days in week amongst us in the cottage. Prabhuji said. 'A genuine holy man thinks whether he can do beneficence to others, spending his life in hardship. But now a days the so called holymen in many towns and cities have not done any help to people, on the other hand they are cheating others. I have confidence in you. I hope, both of you one day will be preachers of our glorious religion and thereby bring the victory flag of humanity flying and be great.' Shravana and myself were listening to Prabhuji intently. We got like finding the source of inspiration from Prabhuji. Having experience and nourishment of life Prabhuji's voice sounded like distinctly visible words.

.... We were visiting pilgrimages moving around. In this way three years passed. Shravana talked on telephone to her home and Mataji once in four or five months. In course of time her talk to her home was after long duration. She never faced trouble in visiting holy places with Prabhuji and me. She also informed at her home that there was no certainty where and when we would stay, hence it would be difficult to talk to them.

Once we had visited some other pilgrimages in India. We visited Prayag, Mathura, Brindaban, Kashi, Puri, Rameswaram and Kanyakumari. We collected details about the places. Prabhuji had not come before, to these places. He did not want to visit before, for the fear of facing difficulties singly. Now he was pleased to move with us. We arrived at New Delhi after moving for two months. The scenery of the seas had made us enchanting. The experience of the mountains in the north and that of the seas in the south took us one step above our knowledge.

In Delhi we entered a big book-shop to buy some books. Shravana purchased three books about Indian Philosophy. Books on Philosophy certainly would help us. To know the functions of the human body, I purchased two books on anatomy and physiology. Shravana and I wanted to buy a thing which Prabhuji would like.

I requested Prabhuji, 'Please, tell us a name of the thing, which you would like. We would like to buy that for you.'

He said, 'I am pleased at your purchases. Take for granted that I have no choice for likeable thing to me at this age.'

I began to think for a while about the thing to purchase for Prabhuji. We purchased shawls and some warm clothes in a nearby shop for all of us. I could not decide to select a thing particularly for Prabhuji. Suddenly I got the sight of a shop nearby of scientific materials. We went to the shop.

Prabhuji asked, 'Why have you come to this shop?'

I replied, 'I have to purchase a special one for you at this shop.'

Shravana also had doubt about what thing I would buy for Prabhuji. I sighted the thing I sought – a binocular. The salesman showed us some brands. Amongst those I had chosen a powerful one. It was somewhat costly, but the salesman assured me, that it was of good quality. I was assured myself after reading the booklet. I purchased the binocular of good quality. It was packed up nicely having a belt to keep it hung on shoulder. I used binocular before also but not one of such good quality of a company. The salesman said, 'You will use it in the Himalayas certainly. Do not allow it to come in contact with water and wipe out dampness. Keep it dry, it will last long.'

I said to Prabhuji, 'We have visited four *dhams*. We have seen scenes of nearby places with naked eyes. But now onwards with the help of the binocular, you will be able to see scenery of very far distant places. We can't go to the high mountains in the Gongotri and the Yamunotry but now you can see, those sights with the binocular.'

Prabhuji said, 'I am pleased that the binocular has been bought for me. But it will be more useful for you. You have purchased a good thing.'

Shravana and I were happy to hear Prabhuji's words. We came out from the shop after payment. We saw three youths with modern clothes were standing near a costly car. They used some vulgar words against Shravana. I was very offended. I stopped and saw angrily towards them. Shravana caught my hand and said, 'Don't talk to those uncivilized youths. They many behave in worst manner.' Seeing us to be silent, they were encouraged. Prabhuji was observing the incident. He walked towards them. Shravana and I had fear with the thought that Prabhuji might be humiliated by them. We proceeded towards him to take him back. Prabhuji uttered nothing. He kept sharp sight on them. After a short while those unruly youths approached Prabhuji and said, 'We are at fault, please forgive us.' Without saying a word Prabhuji walked away with us.

I wanted to know from Prabhuji on the way when we were proceeding to Haridwar from Delhi by bus. I said to him, 'Shravana and I were feared by the thought that you might be disgraced by those evil-minded youths. So, I rushed to you. But they soon begged apology to you.'

Prabhuji said, 'Weapon of mind-power can be used to subdue the evil force. You can achieve by your mind-sight, such power that others will see the power in your eyes and they will surrender to you. This is one way for self defence against evil power. I have acquired only a little power. In future both of you also will be able to acquire those gradually. In the past, many were perished at the rage of hermits. Now, it is seen as imagination. You will research about these matters also in future.'

The vast shape of the sea as well as of the Himalayas brought different experiences for us. We engaged ourselves in study of old scriptures. Parallelly Shravana and I studied the properties of the herbal medicinal plants of the Himalayas. There were many plants from the past in the Himalayas, of which herbal medicine was used as panacea. We sought help and advice from Prabhuji in all spheres. We had succeeded partially in this field. There were still much to do for full success. We were engaged to study many scriptures to know old India. As a student of Philosophy, Shravana was eager to study to know the ancient Indian Philosophy. She was engaged in deep study to gather more knowledge and wisdom.

Shravana once expressed her wish to visit Assam. She heard about the goddess Kamakhya temple. So she was specially interested to visit the temple. I said, 'But in the Kamakhya – temple, there is a custom of sacrificing animals. As offerings to the goddess, in the temple buffalos, goats, ducks and pigeons are sacrificed.' Shravana was frightened. Then she said, 'I did not know about the sacrificial ceremony in the temple of the goddess Kamakhya. Is it not like a slaughter house in the temple? I do not wish ever to visit such a temple. Now in the modern age, at least the superstitions in the name of religion and customs should be removed.'

And the hope of going to Assam was stopped there. Prabhuji was happy for our abandonment of hope to visit a temple where animals are sacrificed.

More than five years had passed after our leaving from Dehradun. Shravana had talked to her home and Mataji after a lapse of four months. They informed us to meet once without fail for an urgent matter. Mataji also informed that Piku wanted to meet me for a particular reason. Shravana told them that she would inform following day about the possible meeting. We discussed with Prabhuji. They also asked us, if we could not meet them, then they would come to meet us in a convenient place. We discussed amongst us for what reason they had called us to Dehradun. We came into conclusion that we would meet Mataji and the rest at the pilgrim house of the very temple at Rishikesh. We did not want to appear at Dehradun with our saffron clothes.

Shravana informed accordingly to Mataji and her home that we would call on them on Sunday of the following week in the pilgrim house at Rishikesh. We were in anxiety to think about meeting them after five years. We did not think of meeting them before. They also did not talk before to call on us in this way. Shravana was only asked occasionally by Mataji and her mother to meet them, but without much enthusiasm. In fact we tried to forget about Dehradun gradually. I even had forgotten of talking to Mataji and Piku.

In the following week, Shravana and I arrived at the particular pilgrim- house with Prabhuji. It was decided that Prabhuji would remain in the pilgrim house but he would not take part in our discussion with them. For, in Prabhuji's presence they would hesitate to talk openly. I thought – they could inform Shravana about the matter on telephone, if it was so important. We knew that Jintu had married three years ago. A year ago, Mataji informed Shravana about the marriage talk of Piku, that was going on. Now perhaps Piku is married! They might not get us to inform about his marriage!

They had arrived at the pilgrim house. Piku had driven the car like before. With him there were Mataji, Aunty and a newly married daughter-in-law. We sat at the guest-room of the pilgrim house. They came there before also. I bowed and touched the feet of Mataji and Aunty. They felt discomfort. Mataji said, 'You are now holy devotees of God. You should not touch our feet.' I said, 'You are our respectables, and you will remain so for us.' Shravana had embraced Mataji and Aunty. Tears flowed from their eyes. They had met their dear daughter Shravana after years. These are tears of pleasure and sorrow.

Introducing us, Mataji said, 'She is Santi, our new daughter-in-law and Piku's better half. It was not possible to find out you to invite for marriage. You also talk on telephone after long period.'

Piku and Santi bowed to us touching my and Shravana's feet. I embraced Piku and Shravana to Santi.

I said, 'Even after getting invitation also, we could not have attended. What you would have felt seeing us in saffron clothes! We are pleased to see here Piku and Santi really.'

Shravana asked Aunty, 'Mother, why you have not taken sister-in-law with you? I would have been pleased to see her once.'

Aunty said, 'There are difficulties now for the daughter-in-law to travel with us.'

Mataji said to me, 'Let us come to actual subject. Piku will tell you everything.'

Piku said, 'Kalkaji, price of our shares in the stock market began to come down. You told to withdraw shares, if there was any possibility of come down of price of shares. I could not get an opportunity to take your advice for, it was not possible to talk to you. So all shares had been sold with profit of several times. I thought, there might be less after long wait.'

'You have done right thing. There are ups and downs in share market. Now, you are alone, so not necessary to take much risk. It is not easy to predict the conditions of the companies. Now you invest the money in your own business.' I said.

'Piku can invest only fifty percent money, the rest is for you. You were the Principal factor in getting so much profit. So, you must accept this fifty percent.' Mataji said.

'What shall I do with this money? This is your money, it will remain with you,' I said.

Mataji said, 'Do not hesitate. If you don't accept the money, Lalaji's soul will not get peace. If you keep the money in saving bank account, it will not yield much. So, let the money be kept in fixed deposit in your name for at least five years. Also you can withdraw when you need. You only sign on Bank papers. This money has been earned honestly. So, do not refuse?'

Then Mataji moving her face towards Aunty said, 'Anjana, tell Shravana now what you want to express.'

Aunty said, 'Shravana, your father opened a Bank account in your name, you know this. Sometimes money is deposited in the account. We saved money for your marriage. But you did not marry. Then, your father kept the money which was for your marriage, in a fixed deposit account in his name. That money has been growing. Now, we want the money to be transferred in your name. Health condition of your father is not good. We will get solace in mind after giving the money to you.' Shravana remained silent.

Mataji asked Piku to bring Bank- papers from the car. Piku took signatures of me and Shravana on some papers. Both of us could not disobey Mataji and Aunty.

'All the certificates of Bank, would remain with Piku. Inform us whenever you need money. Now it is fixed deposit for five years. You can withdraw before if you wish,' said Mataji.

'Why do you speak to us after a gap of so many days? Shravana, I get peace hearing your voice. From now onwards, speak to us once in a month if not once in a week,' said Aunty.

'I shall try. All the places have no provision of facility of telephone connection, where we move and visit,' said Shravana.

Actually, Shravana avoided to speak to them deliberately. She had not made them know that.

'Where from had Piku married? I mean, where is the home of Santi's parents?' I asked Mataji.

'She is from Saharanpur. Piku's elder sister had first chosen her. Then we went to see. Piku was sent later. I said if he had chosen, then only marriage would be finalized. He had chosen the girl and the marriage was solemnized. But he has done a great work,' said Mataji.

'But what does the great work mean?' I asked

'Piku has recognized you as his *'guru'*, said Mataji.

'I am his *'guru'*! what does it mean?' I asked

Mataji said, 'Yes, it is very much true. I do not know, what instinct you filled in Piku. You said, there is nearly no dowry system in your Assam. The family of bridegroom, who demands and accepts dowry, are disliked by the society. Therefore, being your younger brother, will he not obey your advice?

As he wished, we from home also did not talk about dowry. We were happy that he took the decision on his own. Most of the youths are greedy of dowry.'

'I am pleased, that Piku had taken such a bold step.' I said.

'Mataji has said the right thing. From now onwards Kalkaji is the *Guru* and Piku is his disciple. And your relationship is of *Guru* and disciple,' Shravana said.

Piku and Santi smiled. Mataji and Aunty also had smiled reluctantly.

I said, 'Now I have understood why Piku had offered fifty percent of profit of shares as sacrificial fee to me.'

This time I had seen bright smiles on their faces. Shravana had gone to temple to bring *'prasad'*. I said to them, 'Prabhuji also had come with us. He is not here, for, we may hesitate to talk openly in his presence.'

I proceeded to the pilgrim house to call Prabhuji. Shravana already brought *'prasad'* for all. I had returned with Prabhuji. They bowed to Prabhuji touching his feet. I introduced them to Prabhuji. Last time Piku had seen Prabhuji here.

Prabhuji said, 'Do not be aggrieved about your Kalkaji and Shravana.

There is no same path of journey for all. Think that these are wishes of the God.

You love them. In the same way their love and respect to you will remain intact. There may be distance from eyes but not from minds.'

After saying so Prabhuji went to the temple. After taking *'prasad,'* they washed hands and mouths. Then they had visited the temple like they had visited after their arrival time.

At the time of farewell, Shravana and I touched the feet of Mataji and Aunty. Piku and Santi touched my and Shravana's feet. Once again I embraced Piku. And Shravana embraced Santi. Our eyes were moist with tears. They got into car. Piku had driven away the car. We were seeing towards them till the car was out of sight. The moment of farewell was sorrowful. We were silent for some time.

Later we told Prabhuji everything about the coming of Mataji and others. After hearing us, he said, 'You do not want money, but how much they care for you. They have kept money for your security in future only for their pure and selfless love for you. I have also money of a good quantity. I have decided to transfer those in your names. In future you can spend the money in honest cause.'

We had stayed for two days at Rishikesh. And then we went to Haridwar. After spending one week at Haridwar we returned to Debaprayag.

****

Chapter-5

Shravana and myself had been able to move without Prabhuji. If necessary, sometimes, we were able to give speeches in religious gatherings in Hindi and English in different temples. Shravana had learnt enough Assamese language from me.

Again we visited four *'dhams.'* The binocular was used properly. Prabhuji was much delighted with the binocular having used properly. Prabhuji was much delighted with the binocular to see looks of the Nara and the Narayan mountains from Badrinath, Charabari glacier from Kedernath, the Gogotri glacier and the Gomukh from the Gongotri and the Bandarpunch mountain and Champasar glacier from the Yamunotri.

Prabhuji said, 'You have done a great job to take the binocular. It is an act of thrill to see the mountains, peaks, glaciers and other things nearer to us through the binocular.' Prabhuji was joyful to view the moon and the stars in the sky through the binocular. The binocular had become an important thing for us. Prabhuji said, 'You call it a binocular, but I call it 'beyond learning.' The books we purchased in New Delhi, were very useful for us. Fundamental knowledge of the human body and physiology was acquired by me. Books on philosophy were also studied. Our human body consists of some basic elements. But the mind is a source of will–power, memory, intelligence and mentality. Our brain, our mind – a marvelous skill of creation. We have to wait for a very long time to get its full explanation.

The cottage was improved to some extent. Provision of electricity, water, bathroom and lavatory were made. Another two rooms and the kitchen was constructed. The dining room was also made close to the kitchen. Flower and other tree-saplings were planted in the campus. We started religion gatherings in the cottage with some devotees once or twice in a week. Prabhuji and myself used to stay in the cottage sometimes.

One day Prabhuji told us to go to Haridwar with him. He said, 'I want to hand over my responsibility of money in Bank to you. Soon I want to be free from obligation.'

I said to Prabhuji, 'You will live a long life. So, please give us responsibility afterwards. Let the money remain with you at preset.'

Prabhuji said, 'There is no certainty, how long I would live. If any unexpected event happens suddenly to me, there would be no shortage of claimants of my money. I don't want you to keep in crookedness.'

After two days we arrived at Haridwar. His all money was in the Bank at Haridwar. Joint account in my and Shravana's name was opened. Prabhuji's money had been transferred to us. He wanted to close his account.

On our request he agreed to keep it with only small amount of money. For his fixed deposit account, names of Shravana and me had been entered as successors. Our address was given as Prabhuji's address in the pilgrim-house at Haridwar. We had to make our photographs to give to bank. In this chance, we also made a large photograph of Prubhuji in nearby photo-studio and another one with us. We stayed for one week in a pilgrim-house of a temple. The temple where I stayed after coming from Assam, was near the temple we had stayed now. One day I visited that temple. Taking pass books, cheque books and other documents, we returned straightly to Debaprayag via Rishikesh. At the pilgrim-house at Haridwar, Prabhuji said, 'I am now free after giving responsibility of money to you. I would have donated the money to the temple and the pilgrim-house, had I not you come across. I had a doubt in my mind –

'Would my money be spent honestly in the temple and pilgrim-house?'

One week had passed after coming from Haridwar. Prabhuji said, 'The remaining work is to be completed in one or two days.' On my asking, Prabhuji said, 'I have already told you- I do not want you to keep in ambiguity. Men will come to quarrel with, for my piece of land after anything happens to me. Therefore, I want to transfer the land to you. A transfer deed is to be made citing the transfer of the land as gift to you. I shall die in peace after giving my property and money to my son you and daughter Shravana. All my important papers are in my room at the pilgrim-house. I shall give you those papers.'

After two days, Prabhuji had completed the work of transfer of the land to our names. The cottage had become like temple to all of us. One day Prabhuji said, 'Emperor Ashoka vowed not to engage in battle in future, after seeing the pathetic sight of death of solders in the battle of Kalinga. And then he accepted the Buddhism and engaged himself in preaching peace. He sent prince Mahendra and princess Sanghamitra to preach religion in other countries. The Buddhism got spread. Actually, due to conservatism and rigidity of the Hinduism, at that time, the Buddhism got large spread. In the course of time, much relaxation came to the Hinduism and rigidity was softened. Again the Hinduism had got supremacy. Yet, there are tolerance, unity and similarities amongst the Hinduism, the Buddhism, the Sikhism and the Jainism. The Islamism was spread during the rule of the Mughals and the Christianity during the rule of the British in India.'

'There are still many faults in the Hinduism. Differences pertaining to caste and community had impacted badly on our society. Pride of one's lineage is also guilty for this. You like Mahendra and Shravana like Sanghamitra, try to remove the faults of our religion and observe a vow to bring the truth and reality. There will be no shortage of money for you. For this purpose, take our cottage in future as the centre.'

I was listening to Prabhuji attentively. Then I said, 'I think, due to some wrong policies of governments in power, the differences amongst castes in our religion have raised their heads. Governments have been using the interpretation of upper and lower castes for political purposes. There should be only two division, economically backward and the forward. Let the government take steps for the economically weak sections. To day, politics are played with the poor and hungry people.'

I continued,' What kind of dirty politics are played, when hungry one dies of starvation! District administration is ordered to enquire about the cause of death. All know, death occurred due to starvation. But the enquiry report says that the death had occurred due to some unknown disease. Otherwise, district collector would be punished. Many poor people convert to other religion for two times meal. Agents of religion with money in their hands, remain ready to convert others. Then the administration sends report that they have converted on their own will and not at others' incitement. In both reasons, question of integrity and honesty of the government arises. Is there any other country of dirty politics in the world playing with cruel reality? Why a government is afraid of accepting the truth? The reason is, without covering the truth, they have to lose ruling power. This is the real picture of our politics.'

Hearing my words Prbhuji said, 'Political leaders work for their own selves. How many leaders are there working for the country selflessly! Our religion is no more a state religion, now it is the religion of politics. As much as you go into the depth of the country and religion, that much deeply you will be aggrieved.'

I said, 'Indira Gandhi controlled Khalistan – rebellion. Truly she had done a good work. Nobody wanted partition of India again for the Sikhs in the name of religion. But what is happening in Assam and some other states? For the immigration of illegal Bangladeshis in Assam and those other states, they are on way to be in majority. The birth-rates of the Muslims are terribly high. Same condition is also in some states. The state or central government has no well wish and firmness to restrict the illegal immigration in Assam. There is border security force in name but practically the borders are open.'

After a pause I started, 'One worry has frightened me. For the mistake of the Congress Party, India was partitioned on the basis of religion. Now, as per government information the rate at which the Muslims population is increasing, it will be not an improbability if they demand for a separate Muslim state or country. Therefore, specially for Assam, if the state and central governments do not take proper steps now and if that situation arises in future, then these governments must be answerable. At preset, whether state or central government will protect Assam from lakhs of illegal Bangladeshi immigrants or will surrender to them! Time only will tell.'

Prabhuji said, 'You have thought about your dear Assam in that way. But the political parties and leaders want. how to rule and remain in power They will be capturing the rein of power and will go on governing, even striking at the feelings of your indigenous Assamese people. Keep in mind – in the name of democracy, many undemocratic acts are performed.'

For some days our engagements of works were in temple, pilgrim-house and our cottage. In between, Shravana one day came to know after speaking to home at Dehradun, that her father had expired. She was aggrieved and said, 'I was brought up in love by parents from childhood. One day I left them. Now my father had left me for ever.'

I did not find words to console Shravana. Prabhuji said, 'It is natural to be bereaved at the death of your father. He had done the duties of a father. He had kept money for your provision of security. You are pained for no meeting between you for so may days. As you did not want to show your saffron clothes to your father, he also did not want to see you at this dress. His thought was that – you were the same Shravana as before. I think your father had died in peace knowing that Kalkaji and myself were with you. Now don't lament for. I also have to leave you one day.'

Hearing Prabhuji, all the sorrows of Shravana seemed to go away. Again she became normal.

After the week, Prabhuji wanted to visit Badrinath. He said, 'I am old; for the last time I wish to visit Badrinath once. Don't forget to take the 'Beyond- learning.'

Two days before our visit to Badrinath, Shravana and I were talking to Prabhuji at our cottage. Both of us decided not to call him Prabhuji henceforth. I said to him, 'From now onwards we shall not call you Prabhuji.' He had gazed at our faces. I continued, 'We shall call you 'our father' from today. We have done a big mistake not calling you our father. Forgive us, taking as your foolish son and daughter.' Shravana and I touched his feet. He had embraced us with his hands. Tears from emotion had flowed in the eyes of our father. Shravana had wiped tears from his face and made him sitting. There was silence for long time. After being normal he said in fatherly love, 'My children have grown up. From now onwards, I am totally free from paternal indebtness. You have advanced towards the path of full wisdom. You will be able to face the challenge of life bravely.' We saw a bright, coloured glow on our father's face. I said, 'All honour goes to you for whatever knowledge we have achieved till now. You are not only our father but also the spiritual guide.'

We walked from the cottage towards temple. Our cottage had remained as witness of love and affection of father, son and daughter.

In the following week we proceeded to Badrinath with Prabhuji. We stayed there for one week. Prabhuji spent time using the binocular to observe the mountains and peaks. He was busy in observing the creative nature around the temple. He was delighted to view the moon in the moon-lit night and also the temple. He viewed every corner at Badrinath. He was seen much graver than ever. We took part in discussion at religious gatherings in temple. We had left Badrinath after the week.

One fortnight had passed after our return from Badrinath. Calling Shravana and me to his room Prabhuji said, 'I give you all my important papers. These were in my room for so many years. I had been moving places, so I kept papers here. Here, at least, was no fear of losing them. I donated some money to the temple previously. Even now also I donate a little. It is different thing for them who have shortage of money. In all temples and pilgrim-houses the poor may not get service. Many honest or dishonest rich people donate money to the temples. Many temples and *'ashrms'* (pilgrim-houses) make products on their own land. But the numbers of temple authorities running honestly are less. Many so called *gurus* live in luxury. Don't give indulgence to cheating and deceit. Whatever knowledge I have offered to you, apply them properly. Use them for self–defence in danger. Again, I tell you, I had met you on the strength of some virtue.'

Pointing to the tin box he again said, 'It has been remaining there as a mark of memory. There is one or two diaries also. One or two old things are also there. I shall not be displeased if you read them.'

Shravana and I remained motionless. Both of us was seeing to the face of Prabhuji anxiously. I said to him, 'Respected father, today you are speaking to us in this way....'

Prabhuji said, 'People who hanker after money and wealth, suffer from anxiety and insecurity. Many people earn money honestly or dishonestly, but they come to know afterwards that they got show of respect only for their money and wealth. Family- members of people of ill-gotten wealth, enjoyed no doubt, but those people come to know very late that they have lost true bond of love and respect. At the end, they ponder – for whom so much wealth was acquired! Was the money of people attained illegally? Were others cheated? In the long run, they suffer from mental agony. They cry for love and faith from family members or others. They wish death, but death does not come soon. They struggle to get little true love, respect and faith from others. Then they think of sin. They donate much money to temples searching for peace and seek refuge in the '*gurus*' giving big contribution of money. But they do not get peace, they get mirage of peace.'

Prabhuji continued, 'People running after money, never get peace in mind. Many so called holymen and '*gurus*' have polluted our society ad religion for the greed of money. You are fortunate enough. You did not want money, but the pure money has found the actual owner. Now I am very happy. Do no get any anxiety in your minds. I got much peace in mind sitting on the bank of the Alakananda.'

...After two days, on the fifth day of the lunar fortnight, our father and Prabhuji of the '*ashram*' departed to the heavenly abode. Demise of our father had left Shravana and me heart broken. Some supernatural power seemed to bestow us energy to remain patient and firm.

Last rites were performed on the bank of the Alakananda. Ceremonial fire at cremation was lighted by me. All the devotees in the temple and the '*ahsram*' observed ceremony of offerings to the departed soul of our father that is, Prabhuji. Lamps were kept lighted in the temple, pilgrim house and the cottage for several days. All devotees uttered – 'Prabhuji died a voluntary death.' He never told us, but his talks with us before two days of his death, that he 'got peace on the bank of the Alakannda.'

Perhaps, it was the unknown indication to perform his last rites on the bank of the Alakananda.

Death of Prabhuji brought a void for us. In these days, we were able to do all works without fear and anxiety under his protection. Now, Shravana and I had been turned to be destitute. Others cannot feel the grief of a fatherless children. We felt the absence of Prabhuji in the cottage and temple. We could sense his presence in our surroundings.

After one month, we arrived at Rishikesh for ritual immersion of bones of Prabhuji. Shravana talked on telephone to her home at Dehradun from Rishikesh. She informed her mother and Mataji about the death of our Prabhuji. They had to be explained regarding our fatherly relationship with Prabhuji. They wanted to call on us at Rishikesh. Shravana said, 'We shall depart here tomorrow. After few days again we shall come here. Let us talk then openly. We are now dejected.' Next day we returned to Debaprayag.

I received all things of Prabhuji. After one month, Shravana and myself one day opened the old tin-box in our cottage. The box was the pillar of memory of Prabhuji truly. There was an old Photograph with Swati and his wife. Swati's photograph was with school uniform of frock There were some old papers and some old religious books. He handed over the gift-deed of the land to me before. There were also two old diaries. And at the bottom of the box, there was a small packet wrapped up with cloth. It was a small one, but weighty. I was beside Shravana. I asked her to open and see the things. After opening the small packet, she stopped short. We had seen a pair of heavy bracelets of gold. The artistic works on the bracelets were very beautiful. Shrvana hurriedly tied the packet and kept it as before.

I was turning the pages of two diaries leisurely. There was written in between pages without date. I had stopped on one page. There was written – 'I loved Alakananda very much. I did not remarry thinking about Swati.' Shravana gazed at my face. Again I read – kept the pair of the golden bracelets as a mark of memory of Alakananda. I thought – it would be handed over to Swati. But she had left this earth. Then I thought to donate to some temple. Again, I thought over it, should I seek blessings donating the memento, the pair of bracelets of Alakananda? There is no certainty. Someone might take away from temple and use for own. At last I have decided – let the pair of bracelets keep with me till I live. I shall give away to a selfless, loving and trustworthy one, if I meet.'

Both of us were silent. We uttered no word. After turning over some pages, I read the word "Raghuji' but it was marked with a cross. Then there was written – 'Kalkaji and Shravana are truly my son and daughter. In the last part of my life, I had found them. They have become free from greed and self – interest. They are, now, bound with brotherly and sisterly love.'

Shravana's eyes were moist. With faltering voice she said, 'Truly, Prabhuji was our father.' Tears flowed uninterrupted from her eyes. My eyes were also moist. I could not see to her face. I could not control flow of my tears. I turned my face aside. I had a strong confidence that I would not show my tears to others. I tried to hide my tears from Shravana. Suddenly Shravana came to me and wiped my tears from my face with the end of her cloth like the way, one day she wiped Prabhuji's tears. I stared at Shravana. I felt that this was like a bond of our pure affection.

Stillness surrounded us. After a while, I read the last page of the diary. There was written – 'In this life, Kalkaji and Shravana are brother and sister. And they have become holy devotees abandoning worldly concerns. Oh God! In the next birth, I wish to get them as my son and daughter-in-law. According to the substance of the scriptures of our religion, this is possible. So that, I can put the pair of bracelets of Alakananda to my daughter-in-law.'

There the box was in front of us. Shravana and myself remained stationary. Now there was no tears of emotions. Some unknown power had kept us, as if, in meditation. How did Prabhuji imagine all these about us? We began to remember Prabhuji as our father……. Suddenly a shining ray appeared above the box. The ray stopping for few moments on the box, moved towards the door and vanished in the sky. We were spell-bound. After a while I become normal. Shravana still, was meditating mood. I stared at her face and waited for her break of meditation. She returned to reality and asked me, 'Kalakaji, for how much time were we spell-bound condition? Had you seen the ray?'

I replied, 'We had opened the box today, after the death of Prabhuji. We have come to know all the things in the box. Until we opened the box, Prabhuji's sacred soul remained with us. Today his holy soul had departed us. That very ray had guided the sentient soul of our Prabhuji and father, for Salvation.'

Shravana said, 'Prabhuji's soul also had departed us. This box is invaluable for us. How do you keep it in safety now?

I said, 'There is no possibility of theft of the things other than the pair of bracelets. Till now, no one knew about Prabhuji's memorable treasure. Now it is our responsibility. Every object in the box, is invaluable for us.'

The box was kept in the newly bought iron – almirah for the time being. Later we had to think further. Now-a-days two devotees stayed in the cottage. We had to keep faith on them.

Shravana said, 'If we had not performed last rites of Prabhuji on the bank of the Alakananda, we would have been accused. Prabhuji never said that the name of his wife, that is, our mother, was Alaknanda.'

I said, 'when I asked Prabhuji that why he had taken the land on the bank of the Alakananda, he replied otherwise. Now I have come to know that the land and the cottage – all these had been in memory of our mother Alakananda. Temple authority wanted to perform Prabhuji's last rites on the bank of the Ganga, but I defended myself explaining to them, that, Prabhuji had told to do so on the bank of the Alakananda.'

After this, we arrived at temple pilgrim house. Opening of Prabhuji's box and other matters had influenced us deeply. I had spoken to Shravana, in respect of taking immediate step for the safety of Prabhuji's most valuable treasure.

Next day Shravana spoke to Mataji and her mother at Dehradun. Mataji had wanted me to talk on telephone. Shravana had offered the telephone to me. Mataji said, 'Kalkaji, Anjana and myself want to discuss some matters with you. I don't know in what way you take. We are now aged. We waited for several days to talk to you on telephone. We wish to go for pilgrimage once to the Badrinath and the Kedarnath *'dhams'*. We want to visit the holy places with you. You may get inconvenience with us. So, inform in a day or two. Because, we do not know, when and in what pilgrim houses you stay.'

On one hand I felt discomfort in Mataji's talk and on the other hand, I was happy. I said, 'Mataji, I shall speak to you tomorrow in details. When and what way it will be convenient, I shall inform you. Let me discuss with Shravana also.'

At the end of our telephonic talk, I discussed the matter with Shravana. She seemed to be in great uneasiness.

She said to me, 'Shall we be in comfort if they come for pilgrimage? For many years, we had been in distance from them. And now, shall we visit Badrinath and Kedarnath together with them? Why mother and Mataji have decided for pilgrimage suddenly!'

Hearing Shravana's words, I was on the horns of a dilemma. 'If Shravana does not like the visit of Mataji and Aunty, then, will it be proper to tell them not to come?' I thought.

I said to her, 'Shravanaji, we should think about the matter deeply. It is true, that their arrival may give us somewhat discomfort. But, if we discourage them, then Mataji and Aunty will be disappointed. They can come to visit the Badrinath and the Kedarnath with others, if they wish. They have wanted to accompany with us being near and dear ones. How many days they want to stay, they could stay in our cottage openly. Certainly their decision is not a hasty one. They might face inconvenience to inform us before.'

After a thought she said. 'I think, we should be with them in visit to pilgrimage. All the places are known to us. We are to make arrangements of their visit, so that they do not get any difficulty.'

I said, 'I am happy that you are in unanimity. I have another thought in my mind. We are not sure about when and where we shall be moving in places. We cannot keep Prabhuji's valuably thing with us. I think, if we keep it with Piku in Dehradun, it will remain safe. If we lose the pair of bracelets here, Prabhuji's soul will not forgive us. He wished us to make the cottage the heart of our devotion and accomplishment of works. Let it be with Piku, until we make the cottage safe and well protected. Shravanaji, what is your opinion in this matter?'

'You have made a good decision. Now, we have to endeavour to make the cottage a multi-purpose centre according to Prabhuji's wish.' Shravana said.

I thought, why Shravana was not happy in coming visit of Mataji and Aunty! Perhaps, she did not want to show our austere and devoted life to her mother. This might also happen, that Shravana became a devotee leaving behind all love and affection of family and now she wanted to restrain herself from making a relationship with Mataji and her mother in their visit to pilgrimage. I was very hesitant. Next day Shravana said, 'Kalkaji, today you wanted to inform Mataji. It would be better, you speak to her, when and how they would come.'

On Shravana's words, my doubt had ended. She had spoken openly and no more suspicion seemed to be there. I had spoken to Mataji and Aunty on telephone from a booth. As per discussion with Shravana, I informed them to come to the pilgrim-house of the temple at Rishikesh on Sunday of the week. I would arrive at Rishikesh from Debaprayag on Saturday and would return on Sunday morning to Debaprayag with them. I had told them to bring warm clothes and to come on Sunday morning to Rishikesh from Dehradun. Shrabana would remain at Debaprayag. They would be accommodated in our cottage along with us without any difficulty. Shravana and two other devotees would take care of them. I also informed that both of us would accompany them in the pilgrimage.

We were busy in cleansing of the cottage in the days of the week. Then I came to receive them at Rishikesh and to bring to Debaprayag. Shravana had taken out the small packet from Prabhuji's box and told me to take it carefully.

I arrived at Rishikesh in the evening. Accordingly, in the next morning Piku reached with Mataji and Aunty in car at the pilgrim-house. I bowed to Mataji and Aunty. We had met in the guest room of the pilgrim-house and talked.

I said to Mataji,'I want to hand over a valuable thing of our father Prabhuji's life to Piku. Shravana and I have taken the decision after our discussion. We are devotees visiting places. There is no surety, when and which holy place we visit. So, the treasure is not secured in our hand.'

Then I displayed the pair of golden bracelets to them, opening the small packet. Mataji and Aunty stared at the pair of bracelets and then at my face. I said, 'This pair belonged to Prabhuji's departed wife Alakananda. He kept with him as a mark in her memory. At the end we have the charge of the treasure. We are suffering from insecurity. Prabhuji thought to give away to her own daughter Swati. But she suffered at the hands of her greedy parents-in-law for more dowry. And Swati died premature death tragically.'

Silence prevailed on us for a while. Then I broke the silence saying, 'Our Piku has been able to come out free from the poison – tree of dowry.'

Mataji said, 'Lalaji got more confidence in business during the days you had been with him. The other day, Shravana had said rightly – Piku is your disciple and you are his *guru*.'

Mataji and Aunty observed the Pair of bracelets minutely. Aunty said, 'The bracelets are made of more gold. The ornamental work is fantastic.'

Mataji said to Piku, 'Keep the packet in the almirah-locker carefully. Be sure that other persons do not know this. After my return, I shall make arrangement to keep in my bank-locker. Of course, now-a-days bank lockers are also not one hundred per cent secured.'

I tied the packet carefully and gave to Piku. He kept it in his bag with careful hands. Mataji again cautioned Piku to keep the Packet very carefully.

We then proceeded to the car, leaving pilgrim-house. Piku said to me, 'Kalkaji, you drive the car today to the bus stand.'

I said, 'I had not driven car for years. Perhaps, I have forgotten to drive.

Mataji said, 'Kalkaji, people who know how to swim, cannot forget to do so. In the same way, after learning to drive, can someone forget driving? Now-a- days, so many models of car are available in markets. Some of Piku's friends have purchased new models of cars. But he will not take a new car and says that this car will be remaining in use as a memory of Lalaji and you. He will keep it running with what ever repairing work is required. And when it can't be used further, he will keep the car as a memorial at our home.'

I was pleased at Mataji's voice. 'It is required a driving licence to drive a car. But my driving licence ....' I muttered.

'A driving licence is not essential for this little distance,' Piku uttered.

I said, 'A small mistake, few words can make a life's track up side down. Pretty life's movement can be stopped. I can drive this little distance. Suppose, an accident occurs, then many replies are to be given to police. Police wants you to make a mistake, then, they can extract money from you. Sometimes you are forcibly made accept a mistake, though, actually you have not done so.'

Piku was disappointed. He as well as Mataji wanted me to drive the small distance. I had a bag which I suspended on my shoulder. Sometimes I carried the bag by hand, when it was not heavy. I had opened the bag. Inside the bag I kept the important papers and documents in a file. I had searched the driving licence. I never thought that it would be necessary for me one day. I had found my old driving licence in the file. Still there were some years to expire. I got the pleasure to find a lost thing.

I said excitedly to Piku, 'I have found my licence. But there is no similarity of the photograph to me. So, police might catch me. Then, I can tell that I was not a religious devotee at that time.'

Till now there were anxieties on their faces. They were thinking what I was searching for. Now, joyful smiles had come to their faces.

Mataji said, 'I had lost hope that you would drive the car today. You have kept us in suspicion for this time.'

I started the car to run. I was emotional to drive the car after so may years.

I asked nearby Piku, 'How are your works going on along with driving?'

Before he said something, Mataji uttered from the back seat, 'Leave the Dehradun – Mushouri road, he seemed to drive through jungle, if possible.'

Piku smiled. I understood that Piku could drive very well. Again Mataji said, 'But the other day he had hit a street dog.'

I said, 'It would have been hazardous, had the police seen you.'

All of us smiled on my voice. I again said, 'What will others think about me seeing in the saffron clothes?'

Aunty remarked, 'What ever others may think, but it will be difficult for you if police sees you.'

This time smiles had transformed to laughters. I also enjoyed openness.

The car reached at bus station. Piku and myself had unloaded two suit cases and two bags from the car. There was another half an hour time for Debaprayag-bound bus. Mataji said to Piku, 'Go and drive carefully. Keep the packet without others' knowing.'

I had touched the car once. It came to mind, 'In this car I travelled with others, to Dehradun, Rishikesh, Haridwar, Mushouri……'

Baggages were loaded in the bus. Piku bowed and touched the feet of Mataji and Aunty. I embraced Piku and asked him to go and drive with care. We got into bus. The bus was started and began to run. Piku went away after leaving our bus.

There was not much talks amongst us in bus. Mataji and Aunty talked less. They were enthralled at the sights on the banks of the Ganga. They wanted to go to pilgrimage before. But that did not happen. The bus stopped at a place for a while. We washed our hands and faces. Pointing to a bag Mataji told me, 'There are snacks and other eatables. You can take.'

'Not now, let us take something at Debaprayag itself.' I said.

'We also have no desire to take.' Mataji said. They took only water from water-bottle.

After reaching at Debaprayag., we proceeded to the cottage in an autorickshaw. After getting down, I lifted two suitcases by hands. The other two bags were taken by Mataji and Aunty one each. One devotee approached us and helped. There were, in cottage Shravana, devotee Mugdha and other two devotees. Shravana embraced Mataji and Aunty. The scene of union of Mataji and mother and daughter was pleasant to see. It was natural to come out few drops of tears from their eyes.

I said, 'Shravanaji and myself have decided to keep you in our cottage for the memory of our Prabhuji. All of us are supposed to inaugurate our Prabhuji's cottage and its first guests of pilgrims are Mataji and Aunty. Here we can discuss openly.'

Baggages were taken to room. When our two devotees and Mugdha wanted to touch the feet of Mataji and Aunty, they said, 'Not necessary to touch our feet. You are religious devotees. Actually we should touch your feet.' Our two devotees were Shyam and Rajat. They worked in the garden and also were engaged to do other works in our cottage. They also worked in the pilgrim- house and temple. They belonged to this place, they had no greed for money and were faithful. For some days they had looked after the cottage. They had cleansed the rooms along with the kitchen.

Shravana and Mugdha had prepared to cook. Shyam and Rajat were to help them. Had our Prabhuji been living today, amongst us, how much we would have been happy! The cottage was named as 'Holy Cottage'. Scented sticks and resin were burnt. In the frontal big room, the photographs of Prabhuji with his wife Alakananda and daughter Swati were placed on a small table. Snacks and eatables brought by Mataji and Aunty with them from Dehradun, were distributed amongst us by Shravana and Mugdha. Breads (*paratha*) cooked in ghee and mango-pickles were very tasteful to me. They had brought fruits, ghee and also few kilograms of *basmati* rice. It was decided to use practice of fasting on the full moon and the new moon nights like that of the temple pilgrim-house.

At the end of cooking, a small portion of cooked eatables was put on a banana tree leaf and placed in a corner of the premises of he cottage, for offering to the soul of Prabhuji. After a while we had taken our meal. We talked for a while. For our plain living, it was customary for us to sleep on floor. Beddings were made ready in a room for Mataji and Aunty and for Shravana and Mugdha in another room. The box of Prabhuji, was kept carefully. And my baggage and other things were kept in my room. The frontal large room, which we called a 'small hall'. For Shyam and Rajat there was another room. After a thought, I told them to sleep in the small hall. I told that I would also sleep there, for Prabhuji's memory had come to me. They slept in one side of the floor and my bedding was on the other side.

I was sitting out side, under moon-shine on a chair. My eyes were on the sight of the banks of the Alakananda. My view was towards the cremation ground where Prabhuji was cremated at some distance.

I was tired after the journey from Rishikesh to Debaprayag. I wanted to recall the day's happenings. I did not want to sleep. At one time I had become sleepy. Cool and silverly moon-light was glowing outside. I went to sleep keeping the door open. After a while, I felt that someone entered the room and was walking towards me and then stopped near me to say something. I heard, I was told –'You have sent the pair of bracelets to a distant place. They have come for pilgrimage for their fondness of you. Perhaps they will be living in our holy cottage. If they stay, you can move places freely. Bring the pair of the bracelets to holy cottage afterwards.' Someone seemed to go away through the door, I felt. I was awaked. Sitting on bedding I began to think about the hearing voice. The voice seemed to be Prabhuji's. Sacred soul of Prabhuji had come to visit our holy cottage today! I thought – it might be the reaction of my subconscious mind. Feeling came to my mind – the voice was as if, that of Prabhuji!

At morning I had gone to see the banana tree leaf offered to Prabhuji. I had seen the leaf without eatables. It came to my mind – Prabhuji's pious departed soul, truly had appeared last night. Though the happening might be effect of my subconscious mind, but that was true. I, also, was not sure, sending the pair of bracelets to far distance. I also thought – 'Mataji and Aunty may live here.' I had decided to bring back here the pair of bracelet, after their return from pilgrimage. I thought, not to disclose the happening of the last night to Shravana and others. Next day they visited the temple and pilgrim-home.

I had informed Post office about our address of Holy cottage. After two days we departed to Badrinath and Kedarnath. Both the devotees had stayed at the cottage to look after. Mugdha also would come to give casual visit to the cottage.

We spent four days at Badrinath. Mataji and Aunty were very happy to see temple and scenes of mountains. Shravana did not forget to take the binocular. She had shown the scenery of mountains and peaks through the binocular to them. We returned from Badrinath through the banks of the meandering Alakananda and reached at Chameli. From Chameli via Ukhimath we reached Kedarnath through the banks of the Mandakini enjoying lovely natural scenes. Mataji and Aunty were spell-bound. For us also it looked new again. We stayed at Kedarnath for four days. They were very pleased to take bath in Gaurikunda. Kedarnath visit had given them very satisfaction in their minds. They did not feel tired even in long walk.

We returned and reached at Debaprayag after the visits for ten days. Mataji and Aunty had wanted to return to Dehradun after taking rest for one or two days. They thought that, we might face inconvenience in their staying here. I said to them, 'It will be better for you to visit the Gongotri and the Yamunotri at the same time, after taking rest for one week. No one knows what will happen in life. If you wish to visit later on, other dificulties might come then.' Shravana said, 'Kalkaji has said the right thing. If you wish to visit later we are not sure about where and in which pilgrim-houses we would stay then.'

It was decided that we should visit the Gongotri and the Yamunotri after the week. Next day Shravana took Mataji and Aunty to show the temple and the pilgrim-home. They were given a hint about the ways of living of *gurus*, devotees, studies and works in temple and pilgrim home. There was also devotee Mugdha with them. Mataji and Aunty returned to our Holy Cottage with me. At the cottage Mataji asked me about Mugdha, where she had come from and her years of staying in the temple.

I narrated –Mugdha belonged to Delhi. Her father was an ordinary employee. Yet they had a small house with land from grand-father's time. Mugdha was second child out of three children of their parents. Her elder brother took diploma in engineering and was employed at Bhopal. Her father made children educated with much difficulties, and had to spend much money in education of her brother. Money was sent sometimes by elder brother to the father. Good days were running for them. Anyhow Mugdha also was engaged in a small job in a company. Her younger sister also got a small job after. Her elder brother married a girl at Bhopal and he lived there. Sending of money to their home was stopped by him. Connection to family was lost. There was discussion regarding Mugdha's marriage at home. She had to leave her job. She was compelled to remain in office late even without work. One day, out of frustration she left the job.

Her father informed at home that one boy had agreed to marry Mugdha, but had demanded few lakhs of rupees as dowry. Parents had decided that Mugdha and her sister would be given in marriage after selling their house and land. On the question of selling properties, Mugdha raised objection. Her mother said to her, 'In giving you in marriage we shall get peace. Your peace is our peace.' Mugdha was very worried at the thought, 'My parents would live in rental house after sale of this small property of land and house! What would be their condition at last!' She informed her mother about her refusal to marriage. Age was growing up for her. She could understand many things. She again told her mother, 'Well, you would give away the dowry. Is there any guarantee that the family of the bridegroom would not claim the remaining part of money in your hand after the sale of Property?' Her mother could not reply. One day Mugdha said to her mother that she would move away to a temple and pilgrim- home after abandonment of thought of marriage. She again told that her parents should not take pain to search her. She could not bear the wound, if their house of memory was sold.

One day the girl named Mugdha disappeared from the city of Delhi. Seeking liberation from insecurity, uncertainty and dowry-claim, Mugdha one day took shelter in a temple pilgrim-home at Haridwar. She served there for her food and lodging. Gradually Mugdha came to know inner circles of the temple and pilgrim-home. Some buildings are constructed in such shapes, that for ordinary people it was difficult to go in and come out. Several pilgrim homes have been used as places of entertainments. It is a vice in the name of religion. A temple or a pilgrim home is actually a business place. Devotees like Mugdha have to do hard work to meet two time meals. On the other hand functionaries or so called *Gurus* spend luxurious lives. Mugdha under stood- the differences between sages of yore and present self-styled *Gurus* are heaven and earth. Mugdha had lost confidence gradually in the pilgrim homes. But there was no alternative to her. She left her home to seek peace in life and would spend whole life in the cause of religion. Mugdha had known very late that there was a separate region in the name of religion. Many devotees come to visit temples. Many *Gurus* come to the pilgrim-homes to preach message of religion in temples but they live in luxury privately.

Sometimes Prabhuji visited the temple and pilgrim home where Mugdha served. One day she told Prabhuji courageously about her disappointment. After a thought, Prabhuji brought Mugdha here to pilgrim-home. She liked the simple living ways and methods here. Prabhuji was happy to see contentment in Mugdha. More than two years had passed from her living here. She is four or five years younger than Shravana. She has got a good companion in Mugdha. Prabhuji told us to take care of her.

After some quiet moments, Mataji said, 'There is no certainty in life, when and how happenings come. Truly, how difficulties are in the streams of life for some!' At the return of Shravana and Mugdha to our cottage, Mataji and Aunty gazed at Mugdha like their daughter.

With Mataji and Aunty, we first started the journey to the Gongotri. We reached at the

Gongotri from Debaprayag via Tehri. The path from Bhaironghat was not easy. Shravana and myself were habituated in these journeys. Mataji and Aunty had faced some difficulties but they were relieved by the enthusiasm for pilgrimage. In addition to the temple of the goddess Ganga, other nearby holy places were also visited at the Gongotri. We also visited holy springs and took bath. Their minds were full of delight, seeing distant scenes of mountains, peaks and the Gongotri glacier, through the binocular. We were there for four days. At the time of return, we took few bottles of pure water of the Ganga.

After coming back from the Gongotri, we departed to Yamunotri from Dharabu via Borkhat. Here also walking was difficult from Janakichatti. But encouragement reduced all sufferings. We visited the temple of goddess Yamuna at Yamunotri. Here also we stayed for four days. On their wishes, few bottles of pure water of the Yamuna were taken. Shravana and myself had taken few bottles of pure water from the Gongotri and the Yamunotri during our previous visits. The waters of the Gongotri and the Yamunotri are regarded as the purest. Widely spread mountains and green forest of trees in the vast Himalayas, bestow immaculate gladness to all.

We reached at Debaprayag after twelve days visiting the Gongotri and the Yamunotri. Shyam and Rajat were in our Holy Cottage as before. Mugdha also had come to enquire sometimes. Mataji and Aunty were tired somewhat, from the journey. I told them to rest for about a week and then to think to return to their homes. Mataji said, 'You have been suffering for more than one month along with us. Again I do not want to trouble you for another week.' Finally, at the request of Shravana and me, they had agreed to stay at Holy cottage for some days. After the visits to the Badrinath and the Kedarnath and now about the visits to the Gongotri and the Yamunotri, Piku was informed.

I felt, Mataji and Aunty were pleased staying for the week at our Holy cottage. I recalled the incident of the first night of their arrival at our cottage. I said to them, 'Actually, at this age, you should give up worldly attachment of family and pay attention in religious practices.'

Aunty uttered, 'I do not wish to return to Dehradun. But I do not know, what Mataji thinks about.' I thought, that Aunty was waiting for my words.

Mataji said. 'Anjana, I also want to stay here like you. You have no much obligations to your family unlike me. I have obligations in business and responsibility of family on me. I can't stay here in spite of desiring so.'

I had come to Rishikesh with Mataji after one week in the morning. Aunty stayed at Debaprayag in our Holy Cottage. Piku was informed before, regarding our arrival and to bring the pair of bracelets with him to Rishikesh. Mataji and I were waiting at pilgrim home. Piku came alone to take

Mataji in car. I looked Mataji heavy -hearted. Piku gave me the packet of the pair of bracelets. He took us to the bus stand in car. I had to return to Debaprayag the day itself.

At bus stand Mataji told me, 'Inform me after reaching at Debaprayag. Be careful with the pair of bracelets. Also talk to me within this month.'

I replied, 'Yes, Mataji, I shall do.' I bade them good-bye. And I got into Debaprayag bound bus.

It was late at night when I reached at our cottage, after returning from Rishikesh. Shravana and Aunty were worried for my late arrival. At first Shravana and I opened the iron almirah and had taken out the tin box of Prabhuji. The small packet of the pair of bracelets was kept in the box and bowed in reverence. After placing the box inside the alimirah, I felt, as if, the heavy burden had gone away from my head. After taking a light meal I went to sleep in my room. Shyam and Rajat slept in the 'small hall.' Mugdha stayed at the pilgrim home. Aunty and Shravana were in one room. I heard their voice from my room. Shravana and Aunty was talking very earnestly between them. I felt tired due to my journey of the day. I slept a sound sleep. In the morning I thought, sacred soul of our Prabhuji certainly would be satisfied for bringing back the pair of the bracelets to keep in the box and placing in our Holy Cottage.

Due to my late arrival, I could not inform Mataji previous night. I informed her in the following morning. Mataji said to me with offended feeling,

'You should have informed me of your arrival yesterday itself. I was very worried.'

I said, 'Yesterday I reached here late and it was night. So, did not talk to you on telephone. The telephone booth is also not kept open at night.'

Mataji said, 'But you do not forget to talk to me after one month.' Returning to our cottage, I told Shravana and Aunty that Mataji was very worried, for I did not inform her yesterday about my arrival.

Aunty said to me, 'Mataji cares for you. And the pair of the bracelets was with you, therefore, she had the reason to be worried.'

Shravana informed her elder brother Jintu that their mother was reluctant to return to their home for the time being. I told Aunty and Shravana that Mataji wanted me to talk to her after one month.

Aunty remarked, 'Mataji, possibly, wants to come to Holy cottage once again.'

More studies of religious scriptures by Shravana and me were going on in our cottage. Though our relation with the temple and the *ashram* was good, but now it was not so much. The environment in our holy cottage had begun to be homely. Shravana and I were engaged in writings of momentous essays on some special topics.

After one month I talked to Mataji. She said, 'I want to go to your place once again. Now I am busy. Hope, I shall be free after two weeks. Will my go be discomfort to you? How does Anjana feel with you there?'

I replied, 'We shall be very happy, if you come here again. Aunty is happy.'

Mataji said, 'Piku and others also want to go there. I have retrained them saying that, they are now not old enough to visit a place of pilgrimage. They should go about their business.'

I said, 'You have done well to tell Piku like that. He is now youth and he is to care for business. In future, he can come. If you want to come alone, I shall arrive at Rishikesh to take you from there.'

Mataji said, 'Talk to me in a day or two. Then, I shall inform you the date of my departure.'

According to conversation with Mataji, after two weeks Shravana and myself had come to Rishikesh to take Mataji. Mugdha had stayed with Aunty in our cottage. Two devotees were already there. Previous time I returned same day and it was a hard day for me. We reached at Rishikesh one day before and stayed at the 'ashram'. Next day morning, Mataji along with members of family had arrived at Rishikesh. Seeing all of them, we thought, 'This time they have accompanied Mataji for the sake of love and affection.'

All of them had taken their seats in the guest-room of the *'ashram'*. We bowed to Mataji in reverence and exchanged greeting with others. I noticed a shadow of sorrow on their faces. Before my asking, Mataji said 'It took time to settle the matters. I have made three parts of our properties. At present my part will remain with Piku and Rabi. Let us see what happens later.'

'Both of them will be doing their business independently on their own. Rabi had been doing so already. I have handed over the responsibilities of banking and other ownerships. There remains mutual good will between two brothers. But you cannot say, when wicked men come between them to bring troubles. So, everything has been done in black and white. Your bank documents have been with Piku. You can withdraw, whenever you wish. The room which was for you on the second floor, would remain as worship-place as of now.'

Curiosity for Shravana and myself had increased. I asked, 'Mataji, what have you said these? Partition of properties, hand over of ownership! Have you abandoned all obligations of business and home? Without you…!'

Mataji said, 'You, too, had left after the death of Lalaji. Piku and myself had taken the charge of business. Now, there will be no difficulty without me. Piku will be able to run business well.'

'But you have taken a serious decision suddenly. Will you be able to leave your two sons, two daughters-in-law and grandson?' I asked.

'They have to live without me, if I die a sudden death. Therefore, I want to spend in holy places for some days during my living time,' Mataji said.

All eyes had been moist. Nobody uttered anything.

I said, 'Our political leaders want to remain in power until their death. Ministers want to keep some of heir favourite bureaucrats and other officials in service even after the end of retirement age. Not for competency, but for their self interest the service periods are increased in many cases. Now, as Mataji has retired voluntarily from all responsibilities, we should honour her decision.'

Shravana said, 'As Mataji has already taken her final decision, we should not discuss this further. There is not much time for departure of bus. Let us proceed.'

I had taken my bag already from my room. Shravana had a small bag in her. We moved towards the car. All faces looked depressed.

I said, 'All of us can't be accommodated in the car. Let Shravanaji and myself go in an auto-rickshaw to the bus station.'

Mataji said, 'Had you not told Lalaji that this car could accommodate ten people in needs? We are only eight now. You drive, Rabi and Piku will sit in front seat with little discomfort.'

All of us had smiled on Mataji's voice. Mataji's ___ had seated on her lap. I started the car. To make the atmosphere a little light, I spoke, 'All of us are in the car. Police can impose fine on us.'

Ten years old Anku uttered from the lap of Mataji, 'Our friends say that police are bad people.'

On Anku's saying, all of us laughed loudly this time. I said, 'All police people are not bad. There are good police also.'

We arrived at bus-station. Rabi and Piku offloaded Mataji's one big suit- case and two bags from the dickey of the car. After a while Debaprayag bound bus came. They onloaded Mataji's baggage in the bus. They touched Mataji's feet in reverence and bowed to Shravana and me. We boarded bus. Their faces looked dejected. Coming to us, Piku said, 'Kalkaji, please inform us after your reaching.'

Bus started to run. We were seeing towards them till our reach of view. Mataji, too, was sad at the parting.

Our bus stopped at Sibapuri. After getting down, we washed our hands and mouths. We did not take anything in journey. We took only water from our bottles. We boarded an auto-rickshaw at Debaprayag and reached our Holy Cottage. Aunty and Mugdha came out to receive us with smiling faces.

Aunty said with a mild smile, 'This time Mataji's suitcase and bags are bigger. Perhaps, you will remain here permanently!'

Mataji replied, 'If you can live with your daughter, why not myself with my son?'

Aunty uttered eagerly, 'Is it true?'

Shravana replied, 'Yes, Mataji will continue to live here.'

Aunty embraced Mataji delightfully. Smiles shone all on faces including Mataji's.

Now there was family like atmosphere in Holy Cottage. Mugdha and Aunty had taken charge of the kitchen. Shyam and Rajat also were there to help them. Both of them had planted saplings of different flowers and fruit-trees and planted out seedlings of vegetables besides existing ones in the compound. Mataji and Aunty also looked after vegetables and flower gardens. They remained busy in different works also. Shravana and myself now were able to get more time to keep ourselves busy in studies. We had communicated with different religious institutions and centres. Particularly we collected books and papers from Haridwar and also joined religious gatherings in big *ashrams.*

That year there was the arrangement of a big religious congregation at Haridwar. For some days Shravana and I were busy ourselves with preparation of papers on the defects in our religion and conditions in our *'ashrams'*, for reading in the gathering. We completed the work before the beginning of the religious assembly. We left for Haridwar the day before the appointed date. We enlisted our names. We were informed that only four or five minutes of time had been allotted to us to deliver speech. We were disappointed of not getting opportunity to read our laboured extensive essay. After our discussion, Shravana and myself took decision that, main contexts of the principal subject- matter, should be raised distinctly and deeply by me in brief.

Next day in the gathering, when my turn came, I moved to the dais and began to address -

'Learned people, I offer my humble salutation to all in this august gathering. Myself is Kalkaji and Shravanaji has come with me. We are from Debaprayag. We have been allotted four minutes to speak.

'Other than our religion, many religious organizations in India get donations from abroad. Our governments do not want to stop these religious institutions in receiving outside donations and aids. But the matter of financial aid to our religion when comes, the government quotes – 'Ours is a secular country. There is constitutional bar in giving donations and aids to religious organizations,' Many people of other religions in states of India, take names and titles of the Hinduism. Why do they not use their names of their own religion? Perhaps, they have not abandoned our religion from their heart till now. Crores of rupees come to these organizations or trusts as religious aid from other countries and many poor people in our country are converted with the greed of money. Government subsidies are given for the pilgrims to Mecca. Are not these subsidies religious aids? Then, where is secularism in the government? Is it not the double standard policy of government? If a learned person or a politician voices for our religion, he is ridiculed as a communal one. In our own country, the Hindus are oppressed and displaced from the state of Jammu and Kashmir, but the governments are silent.

We should also, deliberate about weakness in our religion. Some so-called *gurus* in our religion have polluted the religion. They are doing business cheating the common people. If they think of doing well to the people, then, why not they arrange assemblages free of cost? What is the necessity to advertise so much in T.V. channels and news papers? They have disgraced our religion. Many ministers, MPs, MLAs and bureaucrats are followers of these so called *gurus* of our religion or other religions. These leaders and bureaucrats run our country!

Now-a-days many *ashrams* have shaped at various places in the name of study of religion. You will be surprised to see the inner sides of some *ashrams*. When the guest-houses are seen with modern provision of luxuries in abundance, doubt comes, these *ashrams* are for studying religion or luxurious hotels! These luxurious *ashrams* are shaped with black money. People having fat resources of black money, become members or share-holders of religious trusts. They get all facilities of pleasures of life in luxurious guest-houses in these *ashrams*. We have forgotten the fundamental purposes of arduous living in the *ashrams* of our religion. Is it not a crime to acquire wealth in the name of religion? Or, the definition of crime will be different!

Thanks to all.

After my speech, I witnessed clapping of applause from the crowd. Getting down from the dais, I came towards Shravana. She stood up and clapped too. Many of them watched me anxiously moving their heads.

Smilingly Shravana said to me, 'I feared you would forget everything on the dais. The speech was very nice?' Smile appeared on my face too. Being overwhelmingly emotional, Shravana kissed my right hand.

In the meeting, it was announced interval for half an hour. Some left their seats and went outside. An elderly person came to us with a lady. Shravana and myself stood up. Introducing himself the person said, 'Myself is Raghabendra Dwibedi. She is my wife, Mrs. Prabha Devi. We are very pleased to hear your speech. I am associated with the publication of books. Previously I had published various books. Now I publish only religious books. Are you not Kalkaji and she is Shravanaji as you said on the dais?'

I replied, 'Yes, I am and she is Shravanaji.'

All of us took our seats. 'You are persons with reading and writing activities in studies of religion. Have you thought about publishing books?' Mr Dwibedi asked.

'We have prepared some essays and discourses based on religion. To read in today's gathering too we had prepared a long essay. But the organizers of the meeting did not allow us to read the essay on the pretext of shortage of time. In stead of that, they allowed us four or five minutes to speak,' I said.

'We come to religious meetings in search of a little mental peace. We want to attend in near and far places. We would have been happy to hear your essay today. We are pleased to meet you. We have a thought to visit the Badrinath. But till now it has not been effective,' He said.

After this he took our address of Debaprayag. We also took their New Delhi's address.

'Have you any schedule of long visit to places at present?' He asked.

'In this month there is no schedule of long visit. Only a schedule is for two days to attend a gathering at Rudraprayag,' I said.

'I shall keep correspondence by letters with you.' He said.

Then, they departed us. A few persons approached us and praised the speech. But two other men appeared to be displeased with me. One of them said,

'It was not proper to criticize our *'ashrams'* so severely.'

I asked, 'Are you associated with those *'ashrams'*?'

Without answering they left us. I said to Shravana, 'These two men are actually agents of the luxurious *ashrams*. Making rich people members or share holders with fat money, these men increase their amount of commission too.'

Shravana said, 'I think, it would be better for us not to be present at meeting after the break. Even now, there is time to catch the Debaprayag- bound bus. If not, we should go to Rishikesh.'

I was happy at her voice. For, I, too, thought to leave the meeting. We had come to bus station. We got the last Debaprayag bound bus. Darkness would fall at reaching, yet we got into bus to depart to Debaprayag.

At Holy Cottage, they were talking, after taking dinner. Mataji and Aunty wanted to enter the kitchen to cook rice or bread for us. I said, 'Anticipating our arrival late, we had taken something at Sibapuri. Don't cook anything for us now.'

After coming from Haridwar, since two days, I was suffering from cold, cough and slight fever. Mataji and Aunty were worried at the thought that my fever might get worse. I had been taking rest in our small hall. Mataji had prepared a hot mixture of black pepper, garlic and other ingredients in a round bottom cup and she gave a massage to my forehead. Aunty had rubbed warm oil on my feet. I wanted them to stop but they did not. Shravana and Mugdha were near me. I was in deep sleep unknowingly. I had awaked early morning. After awaking I had seen, my head was in Mataji's lap. Shravana was sleeping holding Mataji's hand. Aunty and Mugdha, too, were sleeping near me. I was overwhelmed at the sight. I felt as if, a child and all members of the family were worried for my minor illness. But responsibility of the family had rested on me. At the thought of their love and affection for me, I got tranquility.

Since the incident, Shravana and myself had studied essential quality of herbal medicinal plants to keep ourselves healthy.

After ten days, we received a letter from Raghabendra Dwibedi of New Delhi. He wrote that, he would call on us with Prabha Devi at Debaprayag in the coming week. From here they would visit Badrinath. He would consult us about the amenities in the journey. We all had discussed their incoming visit in our cottage.

After a week Mr. Dwibedi arrived at our Holy Cottage with Prabha Devi in the evening. He enquired receiving of the letter in time or not. I said to him that the letter was received in proper time. At the asking of our visit to Rudraprayag I replied that the visit was yet not done.

I said, 'Dwibediji, you seem tired in travelling direct from New Delhi to Debaprayag. Let us talk in full after your rest for some time.'

Mr. Dwibedi and Mrs. Prabha Devi were seated in our front 'small hall.'

Mataji and Aunty were near them.

Mataji said, 'Arrangements of sitting and beds are done on floor here. You may get inconvenient.'

Mr. Dwibedi said, 'Our interest in soft bedding and rich bed stead had disappeared in our lives. We shall be happy with whatever your arrangements.'

I said, 'We place plywood or wooden planks on floor. And tree leaves and grasses which are dried in sun-rays, are laid and covered with sheets to make seats and beds. Thereby coldness also is lessened. Of course, during cold season quilts and woolen blankets are essential.'

As Mr. Dwibedi and his wife were tired of journey, we had taken dinner early. We wanted to discuss next day and went to sleep after taking rest for a while.

Next day Mr. Dwibedi seemed delighted. Perhaps, the weariness of previous day's journey was removed. Both of us were walking in the compound leisurely. His sight was towards the Alakananda. He enquired how the cottage was shaped. I told him a little about Prabhuji and how he started this. After a while we came back to our small hall and sat there.

Shravana and Mugdha had brought breakfast to us. The rest were in the dining room.

At taking breakfast Mr. Dwibedi said, 'After meeting you that day at Haridwar, we returned to New Delhi.'

'We too, left for Debaprayag in break time after meeting you.' I said.

He said,' I made discussion on you with Prabha Devi after reaching home. We were very influenced by your speech of four minutes. There are two reasons in my coming here – firstly, collecting your essays and other writings I want to publish them. Secondly to visit Bardrinath.'

'Badrinath is the holy place. You have come for pilgrimage so, your first purpose is to visit Badrinath.' I said.

'We have stepped firstly at Debaprayag. Will, therefore, not, the purpose at Debaprayag be foremost?' He said smilingly.

I too, smiled at his logic. I said, 'Shravana and myself have completed writings of some essays. But there are still some unfinished works. It will take time to complete. All the works are our joint efforts.'

Mr. Dwibed said, 'Revise the completed writings once. I shall not touch to correct here or there, if it does not demand so. My weakness for publishing religious books, had made me living. I shall continue publishing till my ability permits.'

'How did the publication of religious books only make you help in living?' I asked.

He remained thoughtful for a while. Then he said, 'I have already said, that I had business of publication of books. I had prospered in business. Various books were published from my publication house. Many writers' books became famous. I provided all facilities to my only son in study. Later on, I sent him to the United States of America for higher studies. He was admitted in California University for MBA course. I hoped, he would come back to take charge of my publication house for further growth after taking the degree in MBA. I wished for passing peacefully my remaining days of life in devotional works after retirement.'

There was silence. I thought, his son might not return, for which he got mental distress. Mr. Dwibedi again said, 'But it did not happen as expected. I should not have sent him to the USA. After taking his degree, he settled there and married a girl of other religion. But he did not get peace.'

I said, 'Now-a-days inter-religion marriages of boys and girls, are taken lightly in our society. Perhaps, you could not have been able to take it easily. So, your son was unhappy.'

Mr. Dwibedi went on saying, 'Inter-religion marriage of some one is not the finishing point. Its consequences come differently in married life. Let us take the case of marriage of Indira Gandhi. Nehruji did not agree. Mahatma Gandhiji made him agree in the name of love. And Firoz Gandhi and Indira Gandhi were married. Firoz Gandhi was a Persian, Indira Gandhi a Hindu. Indira Nehru became Indira Gandhi. Today in India, many people think that Indira had taken title 'Gandhi' from Mahatma Gandhi's family-title. At the mention of Nehru-Gandhi families, people recall memory of Indian Freedom Movement of Nehru-Gandhiji's Congress Party. In this matter, Congress party has been somewhat benefitted. Indira Gandhi remained a Hindu! Firoz Khan alias Firoz Gandhi did not convert. It is not unusual to occur conflicts in a family with the practices of two different faiths. I want to speak about courage of Indira Gandhi. She got encouragement from her father Nehru certainly.'

'Generally, Hindu women married to men of other faith, are converted. But in Europe and America it is seen many Hindu boys married to girls of other faith are converted. Perhaps, Indira Gandhi too, would have to remain in family-bound after practicing Persian faith of her husband! Indira Gandhi got reward for her courage. She became Prime Minister of India and was recognized as a brave and successful leader in the World. Nehru was called weak Prime Minister. But his daughter Indira Gandhi had been regarded as a courageous, skilful and timely decision making prime minister. For the wrong advice of her councilors, the decision of proclamation of emergency in the country, was a blot in her skillfulness. Of course, later on she became Prime minister again. Rest of Indira Gandhi's family-members afterwards could not show that much skillfulness and boldness. Although her son Rajib Gandhi became Prime minister.'

I voiced, 'Probably, your son had adopted his wife's religion, so you are unhappy. Is it now proper to think about your son and be in grief?'

He said, 'I was grief-stricken on his changing to wife's religion. But, for the subsequent events I had to remain weeping in my life. Two to four years passed usually. Gradually he had suffered from inferiority complex from his friends' circle. Even his wife's parents and others had used harsh language to him. He was belittled for coming from a country of poors, corrupts and hypocritical *Gurus* like in India. His friends laughed at him speaking about India, a country of casteism and untouchability. He could not take them easily. After hearing all these I had though to bring him back. But, before that he committed suicide. I was informed by his wife's side. When I wanted to bring my son's dead body to New Delhi, they did not prevent much. Finally, the dead body was brought back and funeral rites were performed on the bank of the Yamuna river.'

'Though we were disunited, I wanted my son to spend a healthy and peaceful life. But the death came to him. For us, it was beyond our imagination. I could not pay attention to my business. Publication work was about to be closed. At last on the advice of Prabha Devi, we tried to refrain from all sorts of grief, in publishing some religious books. The other day, after hearing your speech in the religious gathering, I thought that self-criticism of our religion was necessary. People should know about deceivers and cheats running in the name of religion. In these themes, there are not sufficient books or essays. I think it is my duty to encourage you, as you have proceeded somewhat on this topic. Now-a-days I do not think about profit and loss. I shall be fortunate enough in publishing your writings and thereby, serving people a little.'

After hearing Mr. Dwibedi's words I remained speechless. Knowing the incidents in his sorrowful life, I too, was very grieved. How the mental grief of man, changes the stream of life! Mr. Dwibedi was mentally distressed.

I said, 'From our conversation, I have come to know your heart-rending grief. My heart goes with you. I cannot find words to console you. You and Prabha Devi have come here to encourage us. For this, we are grateful to you. We have felt lucky enough for your arrival here.'

In between our conversation, Mataji and others had been sitting near us. With dejected faces all of them sighed. Tears streamed down Prabha Devi's cheeks.

I said, 'Everything is in the hands of the destiny. Your son did a mistake to run after the mirage of momentary pleasure and luxury. He seemed to know his mistake afterwards, for which he killed himself untimely. That dark night has passed, now you are living with the reality of life.'

'This is why our poet sings –

> 'Slowly, slowly doth not shine
> In the evening sky of the East,
> The Full moon, if not
> The dark New moon eclipses her.'

Mr. Dwibedi had repeated the lines of the poem. Then he acclaimed, 'Excellent!'

After taking our midday meal we seated for discussion. Emphasing the visit to the Kedarnath also, I said, 'Dwibediji, it is not sure when you can come again. So, it is better to visit Kedarnath along with Badrinath. Of course, a little difficulty will arise. If possible, you should visit the Gongotri and the Yamunotri also once'

Mr Dwibedi said, 'Well, on your suggestion we shall visit Kedarnath, too, along with Badrinath. It is not now to the Gongotri and the Yamunotri. Let us visit them later on, if we are lucky enough.'

In the evening all of us visited our temple and *ashram*. We spent one hour there. Mr. Dwibedi and Prabha Devi were happy to visit.

After two days firstly we started our journey to visit Badrinath. Mataji and Aunty would remain in Holy-Cottage. Shyam and Rajat also will be there. Mataji said, 'By the grace of the God, we have visited four *dhams*. Now we shall get peace bowing from here.' Mugdha did not visit before. Therefore, Shravana got Mugdha with us this time.

Mr. Dwibedi said, 'We have got the opportunity to visit Badriath with you, by the blessings of the God. Myself and Prabha Devi were anxious about the tiredness of journey to bear with. Now you have added Kedarnath, too. At your presence we are safe. Good fortune prevails upon us.'

I said, 'Shravanaji and myself visited four *dhams* at first with Prabhuji. After then we visited four *dhams* with Mataji and Aunty. All places are known to us.'

We spent five days at Badrinath. We visited the Vishnu temple along with holy places and springs. Mr. Dwibedi and Prabha Devi were highly delighted to see the Badrinath *dham* and natural scenes of the Himalayas. Mugdha also was very glad to visit Badrinath first time.

Then we returned to Chameli and started journey to the Kedarnath *dham* via Ukhimath. Our jorney to Badrinath *dham* was through the banks of the meandering Alakandanda, enjoying scenes bestowed by the nature. Our journey to Kedarnath *dham* was through the meanders on the banks of the Mandakini. They enjoyed the beauty of mountains and green forests. And, their eyes were shining. After taking bath in Gaurikunda, we walked on and reached Kedarnath *dham*. Mr. Dwibedi and Prabha Devi were fat persons. Though they faced some difficulties at first on walking, pleasure of pilgrimage made them to forget tiredness. We stayed for four days at Kedarnath. Here also we remained in *ashram* like that of Badrinath. Weather here was very cold. It was not difficult for Shravana and me. We were habituated to move in cold weather. Care was taken for Mr. Dwibedi and Prabha Devi, so that, they did not suffer from any illness. All of us used warm water. Shravana took care of Mugdha so that, she did not suffer from coldness for her first visit here.

Shravana did not forget to take the binocular to observe the wonderland of the nature. Mr Dwibedi, Prabha Devi and Mugdha enjoyed the beauty of mountains, peaks and glaciers, through the binocular for the first-time. Their bright faces were the expression of delight.

After visiting two *dhams* for twelve days we reached safely at Holy Cottage without any obstacle. Mataji and Aunty were very anxious about us. After our safe return, they were relaxed. Mr. Dwibedi and Prabha Devi, after taking rest for three days, wanted to return to New Delhi. In these days Mr. Dwibedi went over our essays.

I said to him, 'There is only one copy of the essays. Please keep them carefully, so that, these are not lost in printing press.'

He said, 'Don't worry. I shall make photostat of essays after return to New Delhi. Try to complete the work of the remaining essays. I shall be informing you about the progress of publishing in letters.'

I said, 'After meeting you, we have been free from worry. We had wanted to publish our essays from Haridwar. For this, there are engagements and running abouts. We have money but did not want to take burden of publication. We were also worried about what response, we would get from other book publishers. You have relieved us of all worries.'

He said, 'We shall get solace in contributing something to your noble purpose. As these are written in English, I shall try for publicity of essays in outside also.'

After one week from Mr. Dwibedi's return to Delhi, we received one letter written by him. After one month we received another letter. He wrote, 'Composing works of the essays are about to finish. After proof reading, these will be ready for printing within a week. Keeping context of your essays, other two or three discourses also have been included. If everything goes well, the completed book will come out in print within two or three months.'

Shravana and myself were happy in receiving the letter from Mr. Dwibedi. I said to her, 'We have got a great inspiration from Mr. Dwibedi, to write big books at least in our names in future.' Smile appeared on Shravana's face. Mataji, Aunty and Mugdha were informed about Mr. Dwibedi's letter. All of them were full of go. Shravana and myself had begun to compose the other essays with great zeal henceforth.

We received another letter from Mr. Dwibedi after three months. He had invited Shravana and me to their home in Delhi. He also wrote that the book had come out in print. We would be their guests at Delhi and would receive the book.

As per our discussion, Shravana and myself set out to New Delhi, along with Mugdha. Mugdha did not want to go to New Delhi at the beginning. Mataji said to her, 'Don't be in grief for the past. No one now knows you in Delhi. Kalkaji and Shravana will remain with you, therefore, you will not feel any discomfort.' Then only Mugdha agreed to go with us. Actually Mataji sent her with us, so that, she would refresh her mind with the journey.

We reached Mr. Dwibedi's house from ISBT, New Delhi by taxi. Mr. Dwibedi wanted to take us from ISBT by his own car. But we refused politely. We talked on telephone to Mr. Dwibedi from the bus-stand. Therefore, no difficulty for us arose in finding out his house. It was a three-storied big house. Mr. Dwibedi and Prabha Devi were waiting for us at the gate. We bowed to them with folded hands. They, too, reciprocated.

Mr. Dwibedi said, 'We are grateful to you for your arrival at our home.' He took us to upper floor. Ground floor and the second floor are rented. They resided in the first floor. A maid was for cooking and a man for cleaning and marketing along with other household work. We refreshed ourselves after washing our hands and faces. We came to New Delhi direct from Debaprayag. We arrived late afternoon. We were served fruit-juices. Electric light had begun to shine the city of New Delhi With few books in his hand Mr. Dwibedi said, 'Here are your books. Printing quality has been good and the cover picture of the book is related to religion. I do not know what you feel.'

Shravana, Mugdha and myself took a copy each. Pleasure was felt having own names on the book. There were names of Shravana, myself and another one on the cover. Shravana was seen to be happy. We opened the books to read little. There were two other essays besides ours in the book. Our essays in print, we felt differently.

I said to Mr. Dwidbedi, 'Looking at the book, we are pleased. Who is he, whose two essays included along with ours in the book?'

Mr. Dwibedi replied, 'You have seen the name of Mr. Rammohan. He is a great writer and a learned man. Formerly he studied at Kashi. He writes on important topics. Your essays are also on heavy subject. Hence these have been printed together. He, too, has written in English like you. I shall try to publish the Hindi edition of the book later.'

Prabha Devi brought fruits in a platter for us. We took one or two each. I took two bananas. Beddings were arranged for us on floor – one room for me and Mr. Dwibedi and another room for Prabha Devi, Shravana and Mugdha.

Mr. Dwibedi said, 'We are fortunate enough to stay with you. Our rich bedsteads have been stored in a room. Now-a-days we sleep on floor- bedding. Staying together we can talk all about.'

Food was prepared early. Constituents of food were rice, *roti*, pulse curry and vegetable curry. We took our meals sitting on floor. Mr. Dwibedi said, 'There were costly dining table and chairs in this room before. These are row kept in store room. We, too, are trying to lead our lives like you. You are wearers of saffron clothes and we are still not. This is the difference. There are other differences also – you live in your hut Holy Cottage and we live in concrete building, we drive our own car.' Before going to bed we talked a little.

We remained for three days at Mr. Dwibedi's house. He showed us New Delhi in his car driving himself. I asked Mugdha,' Do you want to go to your former home once?'

Mugdha replied, 'I want to forget my past. I do not know who lives now in our house! Most probably, it has been sold only or, the house might be there, but parents died! Is my sister alive? Or, she died being the victim of dowry! Or, she did not sit in marriage! I have no courage to face the harsh reality. Let me live as a member of the family in the Holy Cottage.'

Hearing her voice, Shravana and I remained silent. Shravana embraced her. Tears came out from Mugdha's eyes. Perhaps, it is a sign of happiness of affection for Holy Cottage. Or, a mark of memory of her harsh past!

At the time of our return to Debaprayag I had seen a cheque in Mr. Dwibedi's hand. He said, 'I have paid now this amount of only few thousand of rupees of royalty for your book. I have not written your names on the cheque, for I do not know what exact names are in your bank account. You will write the names by yourselves.'

I said, 'There is a joint bank account in the name of Shravana and me at Haridwar. The names in bank account are different. Shravana's title has been added in her name. My name is totally different. Our individual bank accounts, too, are in other place. Thank you for offering money to us. But we can't take money from you. Till now we do not know what response will be got by our book. This book is our first effort. Hence, we do not wish to accept royalty from you now. We are too happy that our essays have been published along with learned and experienced Mr. Rammohan.'

Mr. Dwibedi said,' Writing matters with standard. Question of age does not arise all the time. To pay royalty is our duty. You do not want to accept royalty. Suppose, this amount is an advance payment for your would-be published book. We had paid advance money to many writers before. Write the names in the cheque. In my private accounts, I have written yours names as Kalkaji and Shravanaji. In future, you will give me the account number of the Bank at Haridwar. I shall deposit direct in your Bank account. Books on religious doctrines are sold well at Haridwar.'

At last we had to accept the cheque. Mr. Dwibedi had dropped us by his car at ISBT, New Delhi. We arrived at Haridwar by bus and deposited the cheque after writing our names at the bank at Haridwar. We got the Debaprayag bound bus and set out our journey. In the bus, Mudgha said to us, 'You have the fruit of labour. As the book is written in English, Mataji and Aunty may not go deeply in it but at least they will understand something. They will feel happy to see the book.' Being emotional, Shravana kissed Mugdha. She was very embarrassed. Mr. Dwibedi told us to bring several copies of the book. We brought only ten copies. Taking one copy, I had begun to turn the pages.

We felt relaxed after the arrival at Debaprayag and entering at our Holy Cottage. Mataji and Aunty were delighted after seeing books in our hands. Mataji said smilingly, 'Now I have seen you to be great leared writers from ascetical lives.' Taking one copy each Mataji and Aunty began to give an overall look.

Aunty said, 'In future, number of your books will go on increasing. It will be letter to arrange another wooden almirah. The previous one is full of your books and papers.'

Mataji said, 'Let the goodess Saraswati bless you.'

Since six months Shravana and I were busy in writing a book on our religion and philosophy. In between, we received a bad news from Mr. Dwibedi through a letter. His wife Prabha Devi died. We thought to be with him at this time of sorrows. Shravana, Mugdha and I arrived at Mr. Dwibedi's house. He said to us, 'Prabha Devi often enquired after you. She said that only for you, we could visit the pilgrimages of Badrinath and Kedarnath nicely. But her one desire remained unfulfilled to visit the Gongotri and the Yamunotri.'

We were listening to Mr. Dwibedi's voice silently. He again said, 'Ours was a wish to meet you once again. But before that, Prabha Devi died suddenly. She left me. Now I am alone. I have decided to form a Trust. For legal works about this, I have discussed with an advocate. I shall remain as the president of the trust till I live. One of my faithful friends has been kept as the executive president. Yourself, Shravanaji and another one have been kept as vice presidents. Two men of my publication-house and other two are members of the Trust. I shall give up all rights of the publication-house. Of course, there will be no obstruction in publishing the book, you are presently writing on religion and philosophy or other books in future.'

I said, 'We are thankful to you for the proposal for our inclusion in your Trust. But we are not able to remain in the Trust. Our ideology was to be visiting freely the Himalayas refraining from the clutch of money and property and from the bondage of the society. We thought to remain without an address. But Prabhuji had made the Cottage for us. He gave away his money and land to us.

On his wish we got an address there. Now Holy Cottage is our address. Please do not give us other responsibility now. Thus is our humble request to you.'

Mr. Dwibedi was on thought for a while. Then he said, 'Not only mine, it was Prabha Devi's wish, too. Now she is no more. So, I cannot accept your request. It is true, people having riches and properties don't get peace in mind. But the root-causes are, thoughts of greediness and accumulation of ill-gotten money. You have no allurement. Thence, you have got courage to speak or write about the wrongs in our society and religion. Invaluable gem is hidden in your austere living. You have mentioned responsibility. Those who want to take responsibility for greed and selfishness, want others to be so. But those, who accepts obligations selflessly and devotedly, attain feelings of pure joy. I hope, you will not distance yourselves from our Trust.'

We were hearing Mr. Dwibedi quietly. We could not refuse his proposal. I said to him, 'You are adorable to us. Your love and affection have made us binding. Just like one day our Prabhuji had made us binding. We can't disagree with you,'

M. Dwibedi said, 'I am happy, that you have accepted my proposal. The ground floor of the house will remain let out as of now. In the first floor, one room is for my use, two rooms for guests like you. Dining room and kitchen are there. One room for the care taker. Drawing room and the attached big room will be used for our Trust. Presently let out second floor will be used as a pilgrim- house in future. There is no surety of my life-time. Hopeful, you have to do the work.'

I turned to Shravana and Mugdha. They were listening to Mr. Dwibedi. I said to Mr. Dwibedi, 'I have a request to you. Shravana and I are proposed to be vice presidents of the Trust, we are happy. Few years ago Mugdha had left Delhi to get rid of the burden of dowry from her parents and took shelter at an *ashram* of a temple at Haridwar seeking liberty. She passed B.A. from Delhi. For the cause of living she stayed at the *ashram* with difficulties. One day, seeing her distressed, Prabhuji took her to Debaprayag. And she remained at the *ashram*. Now she has been staying with us as a member of Holy Cottage. We shall be pleased enough if you include her as a member of the trust.'

Mr. Dwibedi looked at my face for few moments. Then he said, 'One day Mugdha left Delhi. I am happy to remain her in coordination with your Holy Cottage and the Trust. She will be certainly included as a member. Today itself I shall inform the advocate regarding your written names. I want to finish the work of registration soon. The Trust will be in memory of Prabha Devi.'

Next day after preparing all papers, the lawyer showed them to Mr. Dwibedi. Mr. Dwibedi told the lawyer to add a new sub-section in the Constitution of the Trust, where it would be written that, after the death of the present President, either the religious member Kalkaji or Shravanaji would succeed him.

I said to Mr. Dwibedi, 'Shravana and I are devotees moving holy places in the Himalayas. Please do not put heavy liability on us in future. We have been kept as vice presidents, that is enough for us.'

Mr. Swibedi said,' Don't worry. Death will not come so soon to me. To become the president from the vice president is as per rule. Though, you are living in the Himalayas, there will be no difficulty for you in coming for two or three days in a month to Delhi,'

Making the lawyer understood everything Mr. Dwibedi said, 'I shall sit here tomorrow with all members of the Trust. I shall inform all of them today.

All of us should be introduced ourselves. You also remain tomorrow afternoon. Take signatures of all to move the registration-work forward.'

Mr. Dwibedi and I were talking in the sleeping room before going to sleep. Mr. Dwibedi said to me, 'To meet with you at the religious gathering at Haridwar, visit to Badrinath and Kedarnath, experience of staying at Holy Cottage all these things had given me and Prabha Devi an unknown pleasure. Your speech for four minutes at the religious congregation, the lines of the poem of your poet you read at Holy Cottage – attracted us closely to you unknowingly. We have much quantity of gold in our bank – locker. Besides Prabha Devi's own ornaments, she kept much gold with the hope of the marriage of our son. That did not happen. She thought much of things. Those did not come out. She thought of you, too. She thought, it means, she imagined. There is no bar for imagination! She imagined about you and Shravana – you are, as it were, our son and she would have made up Shravana in the dress of our daughter-in-law with all ornaments of gold. The day you had arrived first at our house, Prabha Devi imagined – our son had entered our house with daughter-in-law Shravana. She imagined to welcome you, replacing your saffron clothes by the dress of the bride and bridegroom. These were her imaginations. She had got peace in her mind in the imaginations. I cannot sell the gold, these are related to the memory of Prabha Devi. Once I thought of those to donate to a temple or to a *guru*. Now I have thought, it would have been a big mistake to donate. I have got rid of act of earning virtue by donation. Perhaps, our gold had been waiting for you all these years. I shall hand over those to you. Don't hesitate to sell the gold to invest in noble work after my death.'

Mr. Dwibedi had slept. I was lying on bed, but could not sleep. Many things had begun to come to mind, 'Mataji and Aunty did not want Shravana to wear saffron clothes to be a virtuous devotee. Probably, their son-like love and affection and faith on me, had prevented them to take extreme steps against Shravana. And at last they themselves had come to Holy Cottage. Prabhuji was happy with us as his son and daughter, but he wrote in his diary – he wished us to be his son and daughter-in-law in future birth. Perhaps, Prabhuji, too, was unhappy silently with our saffron dresses and austere lives at this age! Also Mr. Dwibedi and Prabha Devi had imaginations with Shravana and me. I had already decided to make moving in the Himalayas. Shravana, too, had come to my Path. I should have barred Shravana from coming into my path. On my way of rigidity, Prabhuji became a kind of obstruction. Prabhuji had, perhaps, found Swati in Shravana. Therefore, he could not become hard enough on Shravana against coming on my path. But, is Shravana happy truly? Mr. Dwibedi and Prabha Devi had found memory of their lost son, in me. For Shravana only, all of us are living at Holy Cottage like a family. For both of us, a coordination between Debaprayag and Delhi has been established. To think of Shravana unhappy, will be an injustice to her.' I tried to sleep.

Next day the meeting of the trust committee was held at Mr. Dwibedi's house. Mr. Dwibedi presided over. Topic was to discuss the constitution of the trust. Mr. Dwibedi introduced us with others. Perhaps, seeing us in saffron clothes, they had viewed us very anxiously. We bowed to them with folded hands. Then, of course, we had spoken to them openly. At the meeting an ad-hoc committee was approved. And the draft constitution was also approved with slight modification and was accepted. At the meeting the registration work of the Trust was advocated pressingly to be completed without delay. The lawyer had taken signatures of others along with ours on papers. In the meeting, fruit juices were served to all. The meeting ended in a cordial atmosphere at the evening.

After taking rest for a while at the end of the meeting, Shravana, Mugdha and myself stepped to the roof of the building through the staircase. We were sitting there. After a while, Mr. Dwibedi also came there. We were talking for some time. I was looking at the lighted scenes of city of New Delhi. To my mind came the thoughts – 'This New Delhi is the Capital of India, the centre for rule in India and also the centre for exploitation. India got independence. Indians got ruling power, including power of exploitation. Our leaders are owners of money and properties. Corrupt leaders, bureaucrats and business houses together had begun to exploit the poor people of India. Was it an impracticability to make Gandhiji's Ramrajya (ideal realm) into reality" Seeing the woeful conditions of the poor in India, Gadhiji left his turban made of long cloth and used to wear a cap made of little cloth. No other than Gandhiji realised the cries of the poor of India. The poverty of India has been remaining to be a muddy enigma till today. Huge Parliament house, Presidential house with vast compound - these are to remove poverty and corruption in India or to cover up! What the governments have done for the poor and wretched!

I was observing the sky, this universe is full of creating mysteries. Where the universe ends! Scientists say – these were created after a big bang. But how the big bang happened! Scientists are silent. Our Scriptures say, this universe is endless. Scriptures say, our mind is having boundless energy. Prabhuji too said, 'We can do the undoable by the strength of mind.'

My mind began to fly to the sky. At first it had moved to the moon, then after to the sun. Everything is burnt up by the sun, but my mind did not feel hot in the tremendous heat of the sun. My mind began to move through the stars. Sun- like stars in lakhs, are seen in the sky. The mind moved to the Milky way, the innumerable stars with mysterious lustre. Mind began to move in the domain of light. Mind again moved. Again the cluster of stars comes. But in between, there are two or three monstrous creations without light. Probably, these are dead stars. Mind became tired. How far it would cross over! Mind had begun to return. Mind said,' Have seen only very little portion of the universe. This never- ending universe is really mysterious. Where is the end? Perhaps, it will not be possible to explore that.' Weary mind reached the Himalayas after return. After crossing the Kailash, mind reached the Gongotri. Taking pure water of the Ganga at the Gongotri, mind wanted to take rest. At distance, mind had seen the huge rock, sitting on which Bhagirath did ascetic practice to bring the goddess Ganga to the earth. Mind desired to take repose on the rock. Mind was too tired. To climb the lofty rock mind was about to attempt. Suddenly a shout of somebody came from behind – 'don't go upwards, Kalkaji, you will fall down.' The voice was panicky. Mind saw behind, it was Shravana's shriek. Mind came near her and asked, 'How do you know my coming here?' Shravana did not reply. Mind said, 'Let us go back now. Have moved only a small place of the universe. Truly the universe is having no end.'

Hereafter opening my eyes I saw my head was on Shravana's lap. A doctor was nearby. Shravana's face looked panic-stricken and a water pot in Mugdha's hands. Mr. Dwibedi was standing beside with anxiety on his face. Tears from Shravana's eyes made my forehead wet. Mugdha sprinkled my eyes with water. The doctor seemed to be Apu to me and Mugdha to be Aruba. They seemed to come in my trouble.

The doctor said, 'You remained unconscious for some time. Hence Mr. Dwibedi called me urgently. All of them were frightened. Your pulse and blood pressure are normal. Why you remained in the state of unconsciousness, I can't say exactly. We were in thought to take you to hospital. Tell me what discomforts, you feel.'

Shravana made me sit properly by her hands. She had been catching my one hand to keep me comfortable. I said to the doctor, 'I feel no difficulty. For some time, my mind moved to the endless universe. Probably, for that period of time, I was unconscious'

The doctor said, 'By studying scriptures, you know most things about meditation and asceticism. We don't understand those things.' Then he asked me to tell the colours of clothes of others. Being satisfied, he said 'Everything is all right. However, a brain-scanning should be done tomorrow.'

I said, 'Not the brain-scanning, but tell me, if there is any method for mind-scanning.'

The doctor smiled. With his smiling face he said, 'For your mind- scanning, doctors from the Himalayas are to be brought. Well, not tomorrow, but it will be better to do your brain-scanning after one or two days even.'

Seeing smile on the doctor's face, all others' feelings of grief, disappeared. Mr. Dwibedi said, 'Kalkaji, your mind went to know the universe, but you did not know, what situation we faced here.'

I said, 'I had been looking at the sky, with the thought of poverty in India. I don't know, how my mind moved to the moon, to the sun and even to the Milky way.' Then, we along with the doctor came down. We came to the room in the first floor. Mr. Dwibedi accompanied the doctor to the gate to bid him good- bye. Till now, normalcy had not come to Shravana and Mugdha.

Shravana asked me, 'Did you examine something about mind?'

Mr. Dwibedi asked, 'Had certain supernatural power entered into your body?'

I replied, 'I neither examined anything about mind nor any power entered within my body. I was observing the nightly open sky deeply. I did not know why I felt, my mid had been flying to the sky. Thereafter, you had known, what happened.'

Mugdha said, 'Shravanaji's panicky voice had certainly made you return.'

I said to them, what had happened after my mind's return at the Gongotri. They heard my saying enchantingly. Again I said, 'Assume the incident happened to my mind, as an imagination. In ancient days, saints and hermits spent months and years in asceticism without taking food. Modern medical science says, it is impossible. Medical science is more developed now. But, to achieve the analysis of mind, mental power and greatness of wisdom, it will take many miles to go from now.'

Mr. Dwibedi said, 'If it was an imagination, there would have been no necessity to call a doctor. We don't understand the divine power of holy people like you. May be, you are in the line of a true sage.'

I said, 'Myself is not worthy enough of being a sage.'

Next day Mr. Dwibedi took me almost forcibly to a hospital to do my brain scanning. After waiting for few hours the report of my brain-scanning had come. Shadow of anxiety was seen on the faces of Shravana and Mugdha. Taking the report by his hand, Mr. Dwibedi said,' There is no serious difficulty. Everything is working normally. Nothing is to be worried.' All of us felt relieved of anxieties. Smiles returned to the faces of Shravana and Mugdha. Even my own doubt had been cleared.

With smile on his face Mr. Dwibedi said to me, 'Had I not told, you are in line of saints!'

All of us smiled. We were to return to Debaprayag. But due to delay in getting report, it was decided to return next day.

I said to him, 'Dwbediji, your mind is sick without Prabha Devi now. I think, you would feel better to spend few days at Debaprayg with us.' Mr. Dwibedi agreed delightfully.

Following day we arrived at Haridwar. I thought, Mr. Dwibedi might be tired of long journey to Debaprayag today itself. Therefore, we stayed for the night in a known *ashram* at Haridwar. Next day morning we set out for Debaprayag. Our arrival at Holy Cottage, gave relief to Mataji and Aunty. I said to Mr. Dwibedi, 'If you wish to visit the Gongotri and the Yamunotri once, we shall accompany with you.'

Mr. Dwibedi said, 'Prabha Devi wished, but today she is no more. Would it be proper only for myself to visit the Gongotri and the Yamunotri without her.'

Hearing his emotional voice, I thought – Prabha Devi could not fulfill. If one day later on Mr. Dwibedi says that his desire for pilgrimage to the Gongotri and the Yamunotri was not fulfilled, we would feel sad then.'

I said to him, 'Will the soul of Prabha Devi get peace, if you do not visit on an excuse of her absence? After this your age and health may not permit you to visit in future.' On my saying, Mr. Dwibedi consented to visit.

After three days, Mr. Dwibedi, Shravana, Mugdha and myself set out to visit the Gongotri and the Yamunotri. Firstly Mr. Dwibedi and I were to go. Mugdha did not visit the Gongotri and the Yamunotri before. Hence Shravana as well as Mugdha had accompanied us this time. Mr. Dwibedi could not stay for more days from leaving Delhi.

After visiting the Gongotri and the Yamunotri in ten days, we returned to Holy Cottage. Mr. Dwibedi said, 'I have been able to visit pilgrimage of the Gongotri and the Yamunotri with you only by the grace of the God. Recollection of Prabha Devi came to me very much. Had she remained with me in this journey, how much I would have been happy! What the wonderful creation of the nature is – Gogotri – Yamuotri!'

After two days I accompanied Mr. Dwibedi to go to New Delhi. After staying for two days in his house I returned to Debaprayag. We discussed various matters during my stay of two days in Delhi. After return to Holy Cottage, Shravana and I had engaged ourselves in studies.

One day Mataji said to me, 'You did not tell us, we had come only to know from Shravana, you fell ill at Dwibediji's house in Delhi. Had not their worries disappeared only after getting the medical report? Be careful always.' Hearing Mataji's voice of motherly love, I got peace in mind.

Now a days, we went to Delhi time to time. There were works in the Trust. Mr. Dwibedi called us often to spend one week or more in his house in Delhi. He mostly said, 'I have done, I think, a sacred deed, going to pilgrimage to the Gongotri and the Yamunotri with you. I feel sorry, why in Prabha Devi's life time we did not go.' Mr. Dwibedi too came to Holy Cottage and stayed for one or more weeks now.

One day Mataji said to me, 'You said that your journey is not of no-return. Therefore, you go for one day to Dehradun with Shravana. Meet all of them once.' Mataji and Aunty talked sometimes to their homes at Dhradun. Piku informed that our bank certificates had become matured.

Shravana and I, one day, had come to Rishikesh. Next day morning we went to Dehradun. After completing our work in Bank, we returned. We become emotional after meeting members of families of Mataji and Aunty. I went to Piku's shop for a while. Memories of Lalaji came to me. We urged Mataji and Aunty too, to accompany us to Deheradhun. They said,' After going home, we may fall in mundane bondage. For us, it would be difficult to return.'

Our deposits of money in Bank amounted much. Money got from Prabhuji, also had grown many-fold. Shravana and I had discussed, how we can use the money properly. Thought had come to me – that very Mataji and Aunty one day wanted to prevent us from coming to the Himalayas. Now they themselves had left their homes.

I thought,' Let us take Mataji and Aunty to Dehradun one day. Also to Mr. Dwibedi's house in New Delhi once.'

Our relationship with Mr. Dwibedi had been like a member of a family. Once he said to Mugdha,' One day you had left Delhi. Now onwards, think yourself to be a member of our family. Henceforth you are my sister, over and above Kalkaji and Shravanaji.' Pleasant smile appeared on Mugdha's face. It was decided to take a telephone connection at Holy Cottage to facilitate easy communications amongst us.

Writing for our coming book had been finished. There was to make the manuscript completed neatly. Mr. Dwibedi had urged us to complete the work soon, for publishing work. Studies about medicinal plants, too, had been going on.

Mr Dwibedi said, 'I have been aged enough, do not know when the God calls me. Since the death of Prabha Devi, I have had no attraction to mundane things of life. Hence, I have decided to dispose of my property to you by a will. Other things are already there in the Trust's name.'

I said, 'Please do not keep any money and property in our title. We may face trouble in future with the riches. So, give them to some of your relatives by a will.'

Mr. Dwibedi said, 'Relatives! In my days of difficulties, no relative came to help me, now you are only the relatives of mine.'

I refrained myself from asking him about his sorrowful days of the past.

****

Chapter-6

Swamiji felt exhausted in speaking to me for so much time about his past. I did not ask him anything. I had been listening to him silently, just like a speechless listener and the living witness of Swamiji's life-story. After taking long breath for a while, Swamiji said to me, 'Brother, today the recollection of my past life has happened. How and when the life-circles of people take turns! One day, I moved to the Himalayas with the money earned from Lalaji's shop. Thereafter, you have heard my story........'

I said, 'I feel myself lucky enough to my knowing your mysterious memoirs. Sitting here myself beside you, it seems to me to attain virtue, as if, I was going to pilgrimage to four *'dhams'*. I would have been very happy had I seen Shravnaji once.'

After a thought, Swamiji said, 'Me, Shravana and Mugdha went to Delhi for the work of the Trust.

Mr. Dwibedi's health was not good. Both Shravana and Mugdha remained there for some days. I came back to Debaprayag, for Mataji had been unwell. Mr. Dwibedi's health has not improved. Hence Mugdha will remain for another few days in New Delhi. Shravana will come back from New Delhi to this *ashram* at Rishikesh. I had arrived here three days ago. After Shravana's arrival, we shall return to Debaprayag. We have to go to New Delhi, later on, to bring Mugdha.'

Swamiji asked me, 'When will you leave Rishikesh? Shravana is expected to arrive today. Now it is about to be evening. It seems, she may not come today.'

I said, 'I shall spend tomorrow at Rishikesh. Day after tomorrow, I shall depart to Delhi from here itself. At afternoon, from New Delhi I shall depart to Guwahati.'

He said, 'Then, you come here tomorrow afternoon. Meet Shravana, after her return from Delhi.'

I bowed to Swamiji. Taking out the new sweater from my bag and offering to him, I said, 'This is as the mark of memory of my meeting with you.'

He accepted the sweater with smiling face. Bowing to him with folded hands, I took his leave saying 'I shall meet you tomorrow afternoon.' Swamiji accompanied me for few steps.

After reaching hotel, I was sitting on a chair in my room. After a while the hotel boy brought tea for me. After washing my face and hands I took tea. I could not imagine, Swamiji's life had been so obscure and eventful. Along with Swamiji's ascetic life, studies of scriptures, studies on medicinal plants and writings of book are going on smoothly in parallel. Swraswati, the goddess of learning and Lakshmi, the goddess of wealth have both come to the lives of Swamiji and Shravana. To keep themselves away from greed of money and property and to take austere living were their aims and ideals. But money and property itself had come spontaneously to their lives. This money would be used honestly by their hands. This money will make their movement of wisdom full-fledged one day..

Swamiji said many things about the feeling and experience of sorrows and happiness of man in life. He said, 'Sometimes, feelings for sorrow for loved ones are more painful than one's own.'

To my mind, came the thought of Nirala. We had good understanding between us. She had to take liability of her brother and sister after entering the service. Her sister was very talented. She had many dreams with her sister. Talking with Nirala, I wanted to forget my troubled and turbulent days of the past. On my transfer I had to move to other place. I felt Nirala near and dear one.

Several years had passed. Stream of life had changed. I spent some years in service at Imphal and Shillong besides Guwahati. That year, I worked in the office of the Chief General Manager of our department at Guwahati. Officials from different places of Assam, had come to the office. One day an official from Nirala's work-place had come to me for official work. Recollection of Nirala, came to my mind. I asked him about Nirala. Saying 'no question of not knowing her arise' the man even gave me Nirmal's telephone number of her office. For us, it was very easy to find out the telephone number of any person or office in India. But, since these years I had not spoken to Nirala, by finding out her own or office telephone number. I felt guilty. Then I thought, even Nirala had not talked to me since years. Then it came to my mind, how can she find out me to talk with! Next day, I ringed at Nirala's office-telephone number. She herself lifted the telephone.

Hearing my voice, she said, 'After so many years, you have ringed!'

That was the former, same and steady voice of Nirala. I said, 'For not speaking to you, for so many years, I am answerable. How are you? Where is your sister Binu now?'

Nirala said, 'Not necessary to know my news. I am thankful to you for remembering my sister's name. She is most probably, in the heaven'

I had shrieked, 'In the heaven! What do you mean?'

Thereafter, what Nirala said, it hurt me badly. She said, how Binu passed all india service examination with merit after taking degrees with brilliant results. Her first posting was in Arunachal Pradesh. Within the beginning months of her service, she came to know how deeply corruption had rooted there. She tried to stop them. She withheld many spurious bills. Then, came the threat of death from the minister, M.L.A. and contractors. One day, hired hooligans of these corrupt people, murdered Binu and kept the dead body hung from the ceiling of the house. Rumour was circulated, that Binu had committed suicide. Binu wrote to Nirala about the threat of death to her. But so soon, actually Binu would be murdered by somebody, Nirala could not imagine. Case was registered in Police station. But, how far she would run after laws and courts in that unknown place! She knew, Justice would not be done to Binu. How many imaginations she had about Binu! But, everything was lost. She endured the death of her father, death of her brother and then, she had to endure the death of her only sister. I did not enquire grief-stricken Nirala even once. I felt sinning.

Hereafter, I had been lifting the handset of my telephone many times, but refrained myself from speaking to Nirala. I was afraid of enquiring somebody, I might get bad news!

Swamiji's words came to me. He said – 'You have to take much more pains to live with justice than with injustice.'

He also said – 'You are to get courage to fight for virtuousness against vices.' In between my thoughts, the hotel boy entered the room. My thoughts ended there. After taking dinner, I had gone to sleep early.

After getting up from bed at morning, I felt, as if, I had not slept for many days. I walked to the bank of the Ganga. After taking bath in the water of the Ganga, I felt, all my fatigue had gone. I was sitting for about an hour on the bank of the Ganga. Coming back to hotel I took breakfast. Sitting on a chair in the hotel-verandah by myself, I was enjoying the distant beautiful scenes. My vision reached at the temple *ashram* where Swamiji was staying.

At noon after taking my lunch, I took rest for a while. I thought, Shravana might be late in arriving from Delhi. Hence I should go to Swamiji a bit late afternoon. I would have been happy enough to meet Shravana once. Taking my bag by hand, I went out leisurely, with the thought of chatting with Swamiji, to wait for Shravana After a while I reached near Swamiji. He was in his room. I entered his room bowing to him. Reciprocating my bowing he politely told me to take my seat. Swamiji said, 'Yesterday, after your leaving, Shravana arrived at the *'ashram.'* She was late in arrival from Delhi last evening.'

Swamiji came out with me from the room. He made me sit in the guest room and he went to call Shravana from the woman-devotees' house. After a short time, Swamaji came back with Shravana.

Swamiji introduced me to Shravana. Bowing to me she said, 'Honoured brother, accept my thanks.'

I stood up and reciprocated her. We took our seats and began chatting. It had appeared to me - a lustre on the face of some goddess with gazelle-eyes, saffron dress and the lock of long hair. Really! Shravana was like a beautiful and large-eyed goddess – Shravana Devi, a mark of peace.

Shravana said to me, 'Kalkaji had told me about you. Actually, it was decided, we would depart to Debaprayag today morning itself. But Kalkaji asked you to come today afternoon, hence we remained here. Tomorrow morning we shall depart. You had wanted to call on me too. I feel glad for that.'

I said, 'I feel fortunate enough. It seems, you a god and a goddess, who have appeared before me in this earth from the heaven.'

She said, 'Please do not exaggerate much about us. We are learners of path-findings of wisdom till now. Kalkaji is happy on meeting you. He has met one own man to narrate his life. I am, too, happy to meet you today. Till now, we have not visited your beautiful Assam. Hope, we shall visit once in future.'

Swamiji said, 'We thought, would get more time for moving around. But Prabhuji and now Dwibediji, have been guiding us to make engaged in the quest of knowledge.'

I said, 'Let your noble purpose be fulfilled. To save wounded Lakshmana in the battle-field,

Hanuman lifted and brought the whole of the mountain Gandhamardan, as he could not find out the medicinal plant Bishalyakarani. I wish you, along with books on knowledge and philosophy, will, one day discover the elixir vita from the medicinal plants in the Himalayas.'

Shravana brought out a small packet wrapped with cloth from her hand bag and offered to me. Then she said, 'These are some small wooden-pieces of medicinal plant, with various valuable efficaciousness. Keep it carefully in your house. Light lamps and incenses in the day of full-moon. It will keep away your troubles and bring peace to you.'

I took the packet by hand. I asked her, 'Many devotees wear rosary of Rudraksha. What is the effectiveness of it?

Shravana said, 'Many sages wear them in meditation to get peace of mind. Many others also wear them, but to show only.'

I took out the light coloured shawl from my bag and offering to Shravana said, 'I have offered this to you as a symbol of our meeting. Please do not say 'no'.'

Shravana said, 'Can you measure the price of filial piety and brother- sisterly affection? Well, I have accepted the shawl. Yesterday, you have presented a sweater to Kalkaji. Both of them will remain as memorials for us. For whom the shawl was purchased, for your wife or for lady-love?'

Before I replied, Shravana said, 'Please do not forget to purchase another one in New Delhi.'

Swamji and Shravana stared into my face for some time. Then Shravana said, 'Storms in your life had disappeared long past. Now, the message of peace and prosperity is for you.'

There was silence for a while amongst us. Breaking the silence I said, 'I have met you. But it was not possible for me to meet Mataji, Aunty, Mugdha and Dwibediji. I offer well wishes to all of them.'

Shravana said, 'Kalkaji and I will tell them all about you. We cannot express in words how much we are delighted in meeting you. We offer cordial invitation to you to our Holy Cottage at Debaprayag.'

Kalkaji said, 'This way, again we shall come together one day in future. May God bless you with courage to fight against injustice. Let boundless peace come to your life.'

I stood up and bowed to them. They accompanied me to the gate of the temple. At the moment of farewell, Shravana said to me, 'If possible, please come to the pilgrimage to four-*dhams* once.' They bowed to me with folded hands. I reciprocated and bid good-bye to them. I walked to the bathing – place of the river.

Leaving Swamiji and Shravana, I was sitting myself on the bank of the Ganga. The Ganga was flowing silently. To meet Shravana after Kalkaji, it was a big incident to me. The pair of eyes of Shravana brought glimpses to me again and again. I have seen these eye balls, these eye-lids somewhere before! My mind began to move against the stream of the Ganga's water. I wanted to search the tracks of the past.…

I came back to the high school-days from the school days. At the recollection of high school-days, memory of our headmaster sir came to me. Had he been brought to Guwahati immediately after the attack on him by miscreants, our headmaster sir could have been saved. It took few hours to arrange vehicle to bring him. Now I have own vehicle besides my departmental vehicle. These memories bring sometimes mental agony to my heart.

Recollection of college days came to me. The days of Cotton College of three decades ago, began to float in my mind. I had found the brace of eyes like that of Shravana. I had found Tarumala. Whenever I did not see her in our classroom, I thought, she might fall ill! After entering classroom I stared into her eyes once or twice. She also did. No talk had happened between us. Running about for class rooms, to keep busy in practical classes– all these activities made us engaged without allowing thoughts of other things. I was one of the boarders in the hostel 'Third Mess.' Tarumala used to come to college by the road adjacent to our hostel. Some boarders had the habit of eve-teasing. Sometimes they shouted at Tarumala also. I did not know why I felt bad for her. I could not understand myself, eve- teasing is a disease or a bad habit!'

Sometimes it happened so, that she was waiting for me to talk. I thought, let Tarumala talk something first. My voice did not come out. One day it was an incident. There was a guava tree in the compound of our hostel warden. Ripe guava fruits were hanging from the tree. Mohen Malakar was one year senior to me. He was a talented student. He stood within first ten positions in the higher secondary exam. We both went to pluck guava fruits in the evening. Seeing no one nearby, I climbed the tree and Malakar was on ground. I plucked fruits and was giving to him. Suddenly I had seen the daughter of our hostel warden, was standing on the verandah of the quarter. She was seeing us. Being dismayed, I hurriedly got down. Whatever number of guava fruits got, we took in our pockets and escaped quickly.

That day guava fruits were not eaten. We kept them in our drawers. Next day after the end of classes I had come to hostel-room. Malakar had already come. He had no class at afternoon. Taking out guava fruits, we offered some of them to others too. Malakar and I had come to the road-side verandah of the hostel and began to eat guava fruits, sitting on chairs.

'We have done a big mistake yesterday.' I said to Malakar.

'Yes, we should not have stolen the guava fruits. If our warden sir knows, it will be very bad for us.' Malakar said.

'I have said about the mistake after the stealing. We should have given the daughter of our warden some guava fruits.' I said.

'Then, more troubles would have come to us. The girl would have known us very well.' Malakar said.

'Had not the girl wished to take guava fruits like us? Rather, she would have liked us.' I said.

'How do you know the minds of girls? You are a student of science. Do you read psycho-analytic dramas and novels?' Malakar asked me.

'You are a talented student of science. You are busy with the Principles of Einstein and Newton. You also begin to read some of the dramas and poems of Shakespeare.' I replied.

Suddenly I had seen, Tarumala with another class- mate coming on foot by the road. I thought, after the end of classes, they might go to market to buy something. They did not see towards us. For, they had bewared of eve-teasing boarders. Today the eve-teasers were not seen.

I said to Malakar, 'Those two girls are coming. If we give them a fruit each, what do you feel?'

'You want to make us thrashed! Do you want to give pedestrian-girls guava fruits?' Malakar shrieked.

'If you talk lovingly and offer politely, they will not dislike you, they will not be angry with you. The unknown will be the known.' I said.

'I am afraid of speaking to girls. Moreover, they are unknown pedestrian girls. Do you want to invite danger?' Malakar said.

I did not inform Malakar that Tarumala was my classmate. I thought,

'That very Tarumala whom I have not gathered courage to speak openly, how it is possible for me to offer guava fruits to her on street! But I have advised Malakar nicely. Surely, if there is any easiest work in the world, that is 'to give advice to others.' It came to mind, 'Tarumala is near and dear to me. She is very near to me, but yet very far to me.' After the incident of guava fruits, we two did not turn to the way of warden sir for about one month.

Upto our final examination, communication between me and Tarumala continued through the expressions of eyes. After the exam our chances to see or to meet eye to eye ended there. Home-sick students left for home. After some days of exam, I went to Guwahati one day with my elder brother. I had come to our College office. There I met our class mate Shyamalima. She was bosom friend of Tarumala. After slight hesitation, I dared speak to Shyamalima. I said to her, 'Today you have come alone without your friend. Where is your friend?'

Shyamalima was looking at my face for some time. Smilingly she said, 'Will she remain as my friend for ever? She might be friend of some one else. Time waits for none.' Then Shyamalima went away. I was seeing her going. Turning her face back, Shyamalima looked at me and smiled. I began to think, what the deep meaning of Shyamalima's words might be! It seemed me very difficult to understand the differences in interpretation of intelligent Shyamalima's words. Perhaps, Shyamalima knew the unspoken and unseen relation between Tarumala and me! If not, why she had given such significant reply! I firmly refrained myself from more thoughts.

I was very pleased to see our names in news papers. Tarumala got seat at Guwahati and I at Dibrugarh. I thought myself, not now, but in future I shall speak to Tarumala, if we meet. It was new atmosphere for me in medical college. Seeing the long queues of sick people and numbers of patients in wards, I thought, 'Have I done a mistake to come to this unknown realm?' Truly, how the mistake was done by me, I could not imagine. My first time mistake was due to my own negligence. But in second time, how I was detained in practical exam, I could not understand. That remained to me a puzzle. Then, there was one year of incognito living for me. After coming out of the incognito living, I had seen all my hopes and desires lost. Yet, I tried to get a track. The track had changed. I wanted to get college, university degrees at least. I kept myself at distance from the known. I never imagined, I would be lonely in life. I accepted, this is the reality.

It was after four years. One day I was standing on foot-path on the road in front of the college at Guwahati. I had seen, one girl was coming in a rickshaw with some books by her hands. I did not know myself, I was looking at the girl. The rickshaw was approaching. I had seen – this is Tarumala! Fawn-eyed Tarumala! That pair of eyes gazed at me unwinkingly, having big books in medicine by her hand. The rickshaw reached very near to me. I wanted to stop the rickshaw to speak to Tarumala. Had Tarumala said something to the rickshaw-puller? If not, why then the rickshaw was coming so slowly! I could not speak. Some emotional thoughts made me speechless. The rickshaw went past me. Turning her head towards me, Tarumala was staring into me. I, too, gazed on her till the rickshaw was out of sight. I thought, Tarumala too, might be emotional and could not speak like me! It had come to my mind-Some memories in life remain so deeply, 'memory of unexpressed love, love of memory.'

Later on I came to know. After knowing I was grief-stricken, how talented Goda Bhuya left this world for ever after drinking poison in the name of nectar. Miss Chitra was harassed by seniors, Miss Taranga left the medical college for the sake of marriage. Being unable to tolerate deception in love, two doctors committed suicide. Mukut died in a motor-bike accident soon after being a doctor. Once

I thought to find out Tarrumala. But it struck me with the thought – Is Tarumala remained the same girl as she used to be? Or, any mishap might happen to her! If these were known to me, I could not have borne with. Rather, let her remain as a memory in my heart. Our poet says, 'Sometimes recollection of sufferings gives pleasure too.'

I remembered, in course of a discussion, an eminent doctor connected with governmental and non-governmental hospitals one day said, 'Working throughout the day makes tired. I have to remain busy for the service for the people.'

I said, 'Is the service for the people or for your self? You take a fee of rupees two hundred. If the service is for the people, take the fee of rupees ten only. Governemnt is giving you salary. Actually you need more money. Being a renowned doctor, you need a big building, costly car and become a member of a big club like Lions Club after paying some thousands of rupees as subscription. These clubs also get fat donations from many companies. Weekly or monthly lavish lunches and dinners are arranged for the members in starred hotels. On the whole, a position of status symbol comes. You also want more money to make your children educated in costly schools. Your club distributes blankets among beggars at Sukreswar Temple and make them gratified with photographs in news papers and television channels.'

Keeping his hands on head the doctor said, 'Would you make me mad? Helping the poor, the club itself has done the service for the people.'

I said again, 'OK, you have distributed blankets among beggars. But do you know, for how many years the beggars wear these blankets without washing? Are you worried about the spread of the germs of different diseases from these dirty and malodorous blankets? Actually, we want to cover up the reality; reality is always cruel. In fact we want to take credit with artificiality.'

I had seen, keeping his head on the table the doctor began to think over something.

...I could not guess, I had spent so much time on the bank of the Ganga. Thoughts had taken me to the past. Hurriedly I walked towards the hotel. At the arrival the hotel boy asked me why I was late. I said, 'Tomorrow morning I shall leave, hence I had spent the time on the bank of the Ganga.' Events of the day and thoughts made me tired. Immediately after taking dinner I went to bed.

I got up morning at five o'clock. After morning duties I took tea and biscuits brought by the hotel boy. Hotel bills were paid day before. The boy asked previous day an auto-rickshaw driver to attend in time. He put my two bags into the auto-rickshaw.

At bus station I purchased ticket for the New Delhi bound bus and got into. The bus would depart at six o'clock. Sitting in bus, I thought about Swamiji and Shravana – 'No one knows how and when the stream takes changes in life. Best examples of this are Swamiji and Shravana. I wished to see them once more. After seeing Shravana, a chapter of my life was recollected. Where did Shravana's pair of eyes take me?'

The bus was started. Suddenly I could not believe my eyes, I had seen Swamiji and Shravana at a short distance. Probably, they had come to the bus- station to go to Debaprayag. My bus had begun to run. I thought, 'They are two messengers of the God.' I continued to see the two divine messengers till the sight disappeared from me.

'The End'

---- The writer has been able to keep curiosity from the beginning to the end. With the writer, the reader also goes to the fascinating natural scenes of the Himalayas. The reader feels free from the agonies, deceptions in the mechanical life for a while at least. Forgetting all those, reader takes rest in the spiritual cool spheres. Reader has been attracted with the newness of the story and the characters in the novel drawn beautifully.

- Bipin Bhattacharyya, Critic

Printed in the United States
By Bookmasters